The Search

A Novel by:

JANET E. RESSLER

STONEWALL PRESS

PAVING YOUR WAY TO SUCCESS

Printed in the United States of America

Library of Congress Control Number: 2018935589
ISBN: Paperback: 978-1-948172-22-6
        eBook: 978-1-948172-21-9

 STONEWALL PRESS
PAVING YOUR WAY TO SUCCESS

Stonewall Press
363 Paladium Court
Owings Mills, MD 21117
www.stonewallpress.com
1-888-334-0980

CONTENTS

PROLOGUE

If Aaron had not promised his wife, Della that he would take her to Lancaster to Watt and Shand's Department Store for their Spring hat sale he would have gone back to bed. There was a pain in his left chest near his pacemaker that troubled him this morning but he figured it was probably how he slept last night. He sometimes slept on his arm the wrong way and it would be numb for a while. And, Della was already up and dressed with breakfast on the table by the time he showered and shaved so he did not want to disappoint her. He made up his mind to have the doctor check things out next week, though. It would be his monthly appointment with Dr. Sims, the cardiologist.

Della didn't often request a shopping trip to Lancaster and he planned to make it special for her by stopping for lunch at her favorite place to eat on their way home. Della's eyes were bad. She could not see clearly. The doctor called it macular degeneration and there wasn't much to do for it in this year of 1982. So, Aaron and Della became a familiar sight on their trips to the grocery store or to church. She, always holding his arm and advising him on what to buy in the store and they walking side by side up the aisle of Brighton Church to their family pew beside one of the beautiful stained-glass windows for worship. He ever listening and trying to do his best to please her; and they together, inseparable. They had been sweethearts since school days and now when both were past 80 it seemed appropriate that they were seldom apart.

It was Aaron's custom to tell Della what he saw as they drove in to town. He was a retired farmer and very observant. He pointed out certain things such as, who was erecting a new barn, or how many houses in the village of Brighton needed to be painted. On this morning, he didn't feel very well and was unusually quiet until Della said, "You aren't talking to me like usual. What's the matter?"

"I'm just thinking," he said. He quickly regained his usual cheerful way of speaking so as not to worry Della. "Say, you remember I told you that the Lykens' farm auction would be comin' up soon? Well, there's the sign for it... June 30, at the farm!" He made an effort to keep talking. He wanted to appear as normal as possible but the pain in his side was bothering him more and more. He must not tell Della. She would worry.

One of the things he saw ahead was a big tour bus, probably stopped while the passengers visited the Amish house near Willow Street. He started to tell her about it.

"Della, there's a..." and in the silence that followed Della turned to ask him why he'd gone quiet all of a sudden. She could not see that he had slumped over the steering wheel while traveling at a speed of forty miles an hour in their Volkswagen Beetle and that they were careening out of control toward the back of the parked bus.

In the tremendous crash that followed, Aaron died instantly. The coroner said the cause was a medical condition, and his wife died of extensive head injuries an hour afterward in the Emergency Room of Lancaster General Hospital. The local television station, WGAL 8, carried the news that evening of the double tragedy with a picture of the twisted automobile. The headlines of the daily paper the next day carried an account of the accident and showed a picture of Aaron and Della Harrison that had been taken on their 50th wedding anniversary, she, holding his arm.

Folks in Brighton were overcome with indescribable grief at their loss.

CHAPTER ONE

KENT HARTMAN

"Jeff, I'm looking for a Christian woman!"

"If you wait a minute, I'll call her in from the garden," Jeff grinned. From the window where he was standing with his friend, Kent, he could see his wife in her big garden hat with her basket and a pair of shears cutting a bunch of lilacs from the bush in their back yard.

"No!" Kent said, aware of Jeff's teasing remark, "I mean a Christian woman who can be my wife," Kent said. "I've been alone long enough! Don't you agree?" It had been ten years since his wife Jeannine had died of a rare neurological disease. He had suffered through the disease with her in trying to find a cure, in sitting by her bedside in times of her deep depressions, and finally for years secluding himself from all society except his work, following her death.

The tall, handsome, middle-aged man spoke in the quiet of Jeff Cranston's living room with its view through tall windows to the south of an expanse of green lawn. James Kent Hartman had few occasions to visit his friends in the country so when he could get away from the stresses of his work, he enjoyed the peace and quiet of their lovely home in Lancaster County, if only for a few hours.

"Looking for a Christian woman, eh?" Jeff asked as he handed Kent a glass of lemonade from a tray on the coffee table. "Yes, I am!" Kent replied simply.

It was an evening in May, 1982. Fragrant outdoors with the scent of flowering lilac, honeysuckle, and dogwood, and fragrant indoors with the perfume of flowers Jeff's wife, Catherine, had brought in that afternoon, the setting was a delight to the senses. Catherine had arranged vases of dark purple French lilacs and had set them on tables, the mantelpiece, and even on the floor beneath the tall windows. Other sprigs of lilacs in shades of white and pale lavender set off the vibrant rich purple and were pleasant to look upon.

The two men had been friends for a long time. Jeff's wife, Catherine had introduced Kent to her friend Jeannine. They shared a mutual love of sailing and Jeff and Kent and their wives spent many hours together in their sailboat, "Driven by the Wind", off the coast of Lewes, Delaware. There was an open invitation from Jeff and Catherine Cranston to Kent following Jeannine's death, to visit them in Kirkwood, whenever he could possibly get away. A Lancaster business trip had brought Kent south on Routes 283 and 272 to the countryside he had come to love. Jeff had invited Kent to dinner and an overnight stay and now the two men were standing in front of the fire which, in spite of the glorious appearance of the lawn and the late afternoon sunshine through the tall windows, was needed to take the chill from the room. A brisk west wind had cooled the evening, and the warmth of the fire was welcome.

Jeff waited again for a few minutes before he began to gently draw his friend out. "I thought you had found a woman friend. I've known you for quite a while and I know you have never had a problem making female friends!"

"If you mean Claudia," Kent said, "Yes, she is companionable, but in no way could I consider marrying her. You see, my problem is not in finding women as friends. I have met many intelligent, charming women like Claudia. I take them out to dinner; perhaps to the theater. Sometimes, I've taken them to the club for tennis or a swim. I enjoy the company of women and they obviously enjoy me!" Here Kent laughed for the first time since meeting Jeff this evening in Jeff's home.

"So, what's your problem?" Jeff asked, as he stirred the fire and put a fresh log on the andirons, creating a shower of bright sparks, "Is it that you can't find a woman to compare to Jeannine?"

"Jeannine was an unusual woman, Jeff. When she died, a part of me went with her, I suppose. She had all those qualities I mentioned a few minutes ago… wit, charm, a brilliant mind. But, I realize there is a quality missing in all the women I have met since I am single again. It is that unmistakable quality Jeannine had; only a woman who has a personal relationship with Jesus Christ has it!"

"Now we're getting somewhere!" Jeff exclaimed. "Are you trying to tell me you have been seeing women who only appeal to you physically? I'd say that's pretty normal! What about your church as a common meeting ground? Ours has a singles group that meets once a month in the social hall and…"

Kent interrupted with an impatient wave of the hand. "For the first few years after Jeannine's death, I didn't date anyone. I was so reclusive my housekeeper and business associates began to worry about me. It bothered them to see me alone so much. In time, I met Claudia. But to be frank with you, Jeff, it isn't working!"

"Care to tell me why it 'isn't working'?" Jeff asked then.

"It's simple! Our tastes are quite different. Claudia enjoys parties and the social whirl of our society. She loves excitement. In her favor, though, I would say that she is a very religious person. She never misses Sunday morning church services and she gives generously to the work of the Lord."

"Well, there's your answer, Kent. It seems to me you have already found your Christian woman."

"You don't understand, Jeff," Kent asserted. "It isn't a religious woman I need; it is a woman who has a personal relationship with Jesus Christ. Such a woman has an unmistakable radiance about her, a glow that I saw on Jeannine's face many times, even when she was dying! That is what is missing in women like Claudia."

"It seems to be the old 'religion versus personal relationship with Jesus Christ' controversy. Make no mistake about it, Kent, there is a great difference between the two. I'm glad you realize that."

"Well, I do. I must tell Claudia how I feel and I dread doing that. When I return to Pittsburgh, I will meet with her and I will be honest with her. In spite of her interest in me which is very flattering, I must tell her the truth. I cannot consider marrying Claudia."

"By all means, Kent, be honest with her. But doesn't that close the door to a possible pleasant marriage? Surely, a woman like Claudia would do her best to please you as your wife!"

"No. Jeff. I've given this a lot of thought during the past few days. I have made up my mind. To marry Claudia would be to compromise my desire for a Christian woman I can love and who can love me on the basis of our mutual love for Jesus Christ. Religion has nothing to do with it."

"If you had this conversation with an ordinary person of the world, it sure would be confusing. Being religious doesn't necessarily mean having a personal relationship with our Lord Jesus Christ; that's the bottom line. Being religious can mean any number of things; even belief in other gods." Jeff was thoughtful for a moment. He stooped again to replace a log that had fallen forward against the fire screen. When he spoke again, he was very serious. "You have just made me realize what I have in my marriage to Catherine. Of course, the human part of me wants to say that our successful and happy life here is because I'm able to support us well on my salary. To say that is to take the credit from God. The success of our marriage is due to our mutual love for each other within the framework of our individual personal relationships with Jesus Christ!"

"Exactly, Jeff! That's what I had with Jeannine and that's what I want again. Anything less would result in misery to me and whomever I marry!"

"Since you seem to have explored the conventional ways of meeting eligible candidates for marriage," Jeff said with a grin, "What do you want me to do? Aside from introducing you to such a person which I can't do at this moment, what can I do for you?"

"Actually, Jeff, you can do two things for me. You can listen to an idea I have and then you can give me advice. You see, a strange thing happened last evening. If I act upon my first impulse, I may either be extremely wise or extremely foolish. I need your help to decide whether the risk is worth the venture."

"I've never known you to run out on a challenge, Kent," Jeff stated admiringly, though he was puzzled: How does this have anything to do with our conversation thus far? He wondered. Aloud, he said, "Go on. What happened last night?"

"Without being too dramatic about this, Jeff, I will tell you. I was watching the news on the Lancaster television station last night in my hotel room. The newscaster showed a picture of an automobile accident in which both the occupants of the vehicle were killed. The man and his wife were Aaron and Della Harrison of Brighton."

"Yes, I saw that also. The auto accident happened when a Volkswagen crashed into the rear of a parked tour bus that was stopped along the road, awaiting repairs."

"Yes, Jeff. The bus was empty of passengers; and the driver had gotten out of the bus moments before the crash. It was a freak accident, I understand. Both Aaron and Della were killed; he died instantly and she died a few hours later in the hospital never having regained consciousness."

"That happened on Monday afternoon. Today is Thursday. The funeral was to be held today, I believe."

"Yes. The newscaster said that there would also be a memorial service, separate from the funeral. That is to be held from 10 until 2, tomorrow afternoon, Friday, the twenty-first, at their farm." Kent set his empty glass on the tray on the coffee table. He continued, "Which brings me to the point of this whole thing, Jeff."

"I wondered what you were driving at," Jeff remarked, looking intently into his friend's troubled face.

"I met the Harrison's long before I met you, Jeff. They've owned a farm near Brighton for many years. It had been Mr. Harrison's grandfather's farm in the 1800's. I met them more than thirty-five years ago, in the year 1945."

Jeff nodded. He had never met the Harrison's of Brighton, but he perceived that they must be important to his friend in a very special way.

"The Harrison's were very kind to me when I was a young man. Their son, Rob, and I were Army Specialized Training Reserve Program cadets in high school though we lived hundreds of miles apart; Rob here in Lancaster County and I in Pittsburgh. Our paths crossed when we were eighteen years old. We were obligated to continue our cadet training and it happened that we met and were roommates in Virginia Military Institute... VMI, near Blacksburg, Virginia.

"We had no sooner arrived in VMI, it seemed, when WWII ended on August 14, 1945. That was a monumental day to celebrate! The war was over. Japan had surrendered. Everyone was elated! And, we young ASTRP cadets were given the weekend off to go and do whatever we wanted. For Rob, that was easy; he decided to hitchhike home to Brighton in Pennsylvania. But, for me, it was different. I could not go to and return from Pittsburgh in the short time allotted to us. Rob kindly suggested that I should go home with him. And, I accepted, of course."

"So, you, a city slicker, went to the farm, eh?" Jeff grinned, trying to imagine Kent on a farm with cows and corn. "What happened then? Did you return for visits often after that?"

"Yes. Many times. The Harrison's were gracious hosts. The farm was a modest one and did not even have indoor plumbing but what they had they gladly shared with me as their guest."

"Did you continue to keep in touch with them?"

"No. After a few years of visiting them, something happened that changed everything. And we stopped communicating.

"It was only after Jeannine's death in 1972 that I tried to reach them in Brighton. I sent a letter to their old address which was the only one I had. I carefully put my return address on the envelope and mailed it. The letter did not return. They never tried to contact me."

"But I still don't see…"

"The last time I visited the farm was in 1947. I was 20… just a kid, and I had not had this personal relationship with Jesus Christ we talked about; that happened after Jeannine and I were married. We both experienced Christ at about the same time. But that's another story!" Kent's voice was soft as he recalled the marital crisis that had brought Jeannine and him to their knees.

Suspecting that there was a large part of the story as yet untold, Jeff pursued the subject with another question. "Why does the death of these two old people affect you now? They are dead. Rob was obviously not close enough to you to write or to keep in touch. He cannot be of great concern to you now. Or, am I reading you wrong?" He thought a moment, and then, with a sparkle in his eye, he asked, "Did the Harrison's have a daughter?"

"Yes, Jeff. The Harrison's had two daughters. One was a toddler when I was a visitor on the farm. Her name was Sue. The other was a girl in her early teens. Her name was Penny. And, to be honest, it was Penny who became my reason to visit the Harrison's."

"I see." Jeff was again thoughtful. "Have you kept in touch with her?"

"I have not seen or heard from Penny since I wrote to her of my engagement to Jeannine, except for a letter of congratulations from her soon after that. The last time we saw each other was in 1947 after I had visited the Harrison farm for two years, off and on.

"Her parents, though, suspected that we were becoming serious, and refused to let me visit them again. I acquiesced. Penny and I agreed to see other young people. She met a young man in high school whom she later married after graduating from nursing school, and I met Jeannine. In my last letter to Penny I told her of my engagement to Jeannine. I received a letter of congratulations from her in which she told me about the young man she was seeing, and then… nothing!

"As Rob was moved to another post, I was moved to a station in Maryland and was not far from Lancaster County and Brighton. You see, in my many visits to the Harrison's home, I fell in love with Penny. I kept my feelings to myself since she was much younger than I. She was 16 in 1947 and I was 20. She never knew my true affection for her because we kept our letters very open and fun. I tried to be a gentleman though I failed sometimes. She regarded me as a big brother and Penny was a sister to me.

"Hmmm," Jeff mused. "That's understandable. After all, she could hardly correspond with a man who was going to marry a woman she had never met."

"Of course!" Kent agreed. "We dropped out of each other's lives. From the newspaper account of the Harrison's accident, I now know that she lives near Harrisburg, Rob lives in New York City, and Sue is still in the vicinity of Brighton. All of this information was in the newspaper. Penny is now Mrs. Samuel Carson. That's all I know."

Jeff continued to be thoughtful while his friend went on.

"When I heard the news, I thought that I could cancel my appointments today and attend the funeral. But I knew that if I changed those plans, it would be months before other business arrangements could be made. So, I decided to keep that appointment this morning and at least get to visit you and Catherine this evening and ask your advice about attending the memorial service tomorrow."

"Why don't you? You will undoubtedly see Rob, Sue, and Penny then."

"I can do that. But my time here is very short. I must return to Pittsburgh tomorrow evening at the latest. The last flight from Harrisburg airport is seven o'clock. Considering that the memorial service is from 10 until 2 at the farm, I can leave Brighton at 4:30 and be in Harrisburg to grab a sandwich somewhere and catch my flight in time. That doesn't leave much time for a visit but I can attend the memorial service, express my sympathy to them, and leave."

"If you leave here at 8 tomorrow morning you will be in Brighton in time for the service. I will give you directions from here to Brighton. I know you will recognize the way back to Lancaster from there. Things haven't changed much in thirty-five years."

"I thought of returning without making any contact with them at all, Jeff. Suppose they should not remember me?" Kent wavered. Then, with new determination, he said, "I must resolve this matter. I want to see Penny again."

"Have you thought of what you will say to her husband? Surely he will be with her."

"We are mature people. I will meet him and renew my acquaintance with Rob, Sue, and Penny if only for the few moments we have there. I know that I will be given the words to say."

"I see that you have made up your mind, Kent. And, I see that an old spark is still smoldering in the ashes. Who knows but what our visit was providential this time? Do you want me to go with you?"

"No, thanks, Jeff, this is something I must do alone. I have a desire to walk on the old farm land again, too. It will probably be the last time I will have the opportunity to do that. I must go alone."

"You asked me for advice when we began our conversation. There is only one thing that I can advise you to do and that is to pray for guidance and wisdom. Commit your way to the Lord and He will direct your paths, as the scriptures say. I believe in the sovereignty of

God. He may have had more than one reason for your welcome visit to our home."

Just then, Catherine appeared in the doorway. "You two must have voracious appetites after all that serious conversation! Jeff and I are so glad you can have dinner and spend the night with us, Kent. We have breakfast at six thirty so there will be some time, I hope, for you to fill us in on what's been happening in your life!"

In the morning, after eating a hearty breakfast, having a genial conversation with his friends, and expressing sincere thanks for their hospitality, Kent said goodbye to his friends and drove toward Brighton, remembering Jeff's warm handshake and his words, "God bless you in your search, Kent."

CHAPTER TWO

LOCUST HILL

Unfortunately for Kent, the directions Jeff gave him did not allow time for a detour that took him miles out of his way and made him late for the memorial service held at the farm. The actual memorial service was held from 10 to 11 with afternoon gathering at the farmhouse. He could have met the family directly after 11 o'clock but now family members were scattered among their guests; friends and family mingled together. He decided to stick around until there was an opportunity to meet Rob, Sue, and Penny together.

He had parked his car in the lane and walked the short distance to the house where the crowd of friends of Aaron and Della Harrison had gathered. He mingled there until, growing uncomfortable in the press of people, he excused himself from the nearest person and walked out onto the side porch.

Standing with his hand on the banister, he could look far out over the greening fields toward the hills of York County. It was a warm afternoon with a soft south wind blowing.

He could hear the sounds of subdued laughter and the chatter of country people, neighbors of the Harrison's, gathered in the dining room, behind him. He had asked permission to walk on the land of the woman who seemed to be in charge. She told him that Rob was on an errand and that Penny had gone to a neighbor's for lunch. She assured him they would return in a short time. She told him that he would be welcome to walk on the land as he requested. Before he could answer her with much more than "Thanks", an elderly woman bustled up to her with an air of importance and Kent moved away quickly.

He signed the guest register then and realized as he did so that no one knew him. No one gave even a hint of recognition as he walked down the steps to the lane.

There he met a young boy who said, "Hullo, Mister!" He asked the boy if there were cows in the meadow, a silly question but a practical one since he recalled being chased by a heifer once on one of his frequent visits to the farm. The boy answered that there were no cows in the meadow or the barn.

"This place ain't had no animals on it for a long time, Mister. Mr. Harrison, he was too old to farm or have animals, or anything. I reckon he just liked to look at the land. He didn't keep no animals. Cows, pigs, nothin'! No, sir!"

With a nod of his head, the boy left Kent and ran to join his parents as they walked across the lawn toward their ancient car parked in the driveway near the house.

Kent walked along the dusty lane past the barn bridge, around the barn, past a catalpa tree with its fragrant, bugle-shaped purple flowers, through the gate that complained on rusty hinges, and continued along a marshy path to the meadow beyond. He had to step carefully on clumps of grass to prevent sinking into the mud. A spring had opened up here and the water came to the surface only in this spot.

This looks familiar, he thought. He remembered that the field to his right across the barbed-wire fence was the same field he had walked with Penny and her Dad on the first day he visited this place.

That was an August morning in 1945 and the field was planted in corn that was as high as his shoulders. He knew nothing about farms then or the crops grown on them. He asked questions of Mr. Harrison who patiently answered them. Penny accompanied them on that walk. She was just a kid of fourteen and he remembered she wore a pink pinafore and that her arms looked like she had been out in the sun a lot. Once on their walk through the field, she ran ahead and hid in the tall corn, jumping out at them, mischievously. She knew a lot about farming, and it amused her that Kent had no idea how much work there was to do on even a small farm of less than one hundred acres such as theirs.

Now, yellow butterflies swarmed in patches of sunlight where tufts of lush grass covered the hillside up which he walked. He stopped midway up the hill and began a straight course toward a grove of trees several yards away.

He tried to recall what the Harrison's called that grove of trees. "Maple Grove?" He pondered the name. It didn't sound right. "Maple Hill?" That didn't sound right, either. Finally, he said aloud, "Locust Hill! That's it!"

He stopped for a moment to look ahead at the grove of tall, skinny trees. He began to walk more quickly, remembering that there was a beautiful stream in the grove. He wondered if it was still the sparkling, pleasantly noisy creek on whose surface he and Penny had skipped round flat stones. They had contests to see who would get the most skips from a stone. Such a simple pleasure! But times were simpler then, he mused.

Drawing near to the stream, he saw that it was indeed as he remembered. And, a few feet upstream, there was the wide and shallow place where Dad Harrison sometimes drove his cows to the "far pasture". That's where we used to skip stones, Kent said to himself.

He entered Locust Hill and stood in the shade of the towering trees. Overhead, through new leaves, he could see the brilliant blue of the sky. Where had he seen such unspoiled beauty before? Though he had traveled around the world many times in the intervening years and had seen many lovely places, he thought that he had not seen any place so beautiful as this.

He stopped again. This time he looked back toward the farmhouse. It was high above him on a little rise of land. He recalled his first impression of the farmhouse was that it had eyes and could see. Those eyes seemed to follow him and Penny as they walked in the meadow when they were young. It was like that now. He saw the great windows on the south side of the house, wide open and staring at him.

"Stare at me, you old house! Keep watch over the land. You'll find I haven't come to harm anything!" He laughed at himself, good-naturedly. It was so good to be out here in the fresh air. It was exhilarating with the bright sun, the warm, sweet breeze and the brilliant colors of grass and sky acting joyously upon his spirit.

There were the sounds of the stream and of bees humming around the meadow flowers, especially the few lingering violets and Star-of-Bethlehem. He knew that daisies, marsh marigolds, and honeysuckle, would soon follow them and bloom among the grasses; and there was the sound of songbirds. One of the birds flew to the top of a sycamore tree by the creek and called to him from its perch.

"Okay," he said to the bird as if it had given him a command, "I will take off my coat. But only for you, you charmer! Anyway, it's hot! I'll say this for you, little bird, you have a very pretty place to live. What a lovely spot. Tell me, have you seen Penny anywhere?" As if in answer, the bird took flight, its wings beating the air, and its orange feathers flashing.

"Fly on, you charmer!" Kent exclaimed as he loosened his tie. "Maybe I'll find her myself, even without your help."

The hills and valleys of Locust Hill were such that a moment more and he had walked beyond the farmhouse's scowling windows. As far as he could see, there was neither a house nor barn nor human being. All was grass and flowers and now the tall trees of Locust Hill, the gurgling stream and a well-worn path through the grove.

It was mid-afternoon. Two o'clock. There was plenty of time to walk. He had all afternoon, really. His plane departed from Harrisburg at seven o'clock. Even if he left the farmhouse at five-thirty, he would have plenty of time to make his connections. He decided not to worry about time but just enjoy himself in this solitude.

He remembered that if he crossed that little hillock, and walked a little way on the meadow there, he would be only a short distance from the road that led back to the farmhouse. The path made a complete circle and would get him back in time to visit with Rob and Penny, and Sue, perhaps.

He stood perfectly still and felt the tensions drain from him in the peace of this tranquil spot. He breathed in the beauty of the moment. Nearby was a fallen log. He sat down and surveyed the land with his senses.

May in rural Pennsylvania is a sensuous time. There is the smell of the fresh-turned earth, flowers, and new grass. There is the freshness of blue and green. There is the sound of birds and running streams and whispering wind through the branches of tall trees. Over all, on this May afternoon, there was the brilliant light of a warm sun shining through green foliage.

At that moment, Kent felt that he was part of the land, the sky, and the bright water sparkling as it flowed to the Susquehanna River miles away. He wondered how the water of the stream would feel on his bare feet.

"Once I might have taken off my shoes and waded in that stream. That was a long time ago; when I was a boy."

CHAPTER THREE

LUNCH WITH IDA

When Ida Blair invited Penny to lunch on Friday she sensed reluctance in her friend.

"I know you'll be busy with the guests, but you will need a break by that time. An hour or two will refresh you. You know what a strain all that family talk can be." So Ida had insisted and on the day of the memorial service Penny was glad she had accepted her friend's kind offer. She would leave at 11:30 after greeting their guests and before mingling with the crowd.

It was just before noon when Penny knocked at the kitchen door of the neat little house nestled under the hillside within a short brisk walk from her parent's farmhouse.

"Penny! My, it's good to see you!" Ida exclaimed as she opened the screen door. "Come in! Come in!"

Penny hugged her dear friend fondly.

"I'm glad you asked me to come, Ida. You are right… it has become a bit too much for me. Sue is handling things well as she always does and no one will miss me. Besides, tonight when I stay in the empty farmhouse again will be the difficult time. Memorial services are lovely, I suppose, but it brings everything back to me: The accident that took Mother and Daddy from me all at once; all the questions to answer over and over; the funeral arrangements; trying to keep everything going at home and here at the farm. I have begun to tire of it all. I dread the overnight stay in the farmhouse with Mother and Daddy gone but there is a family meeting tomorrow and I must attend. I will be glad when all the excitement is past."

Ida searched Penny's face for signs of strain. There were shadows under the dark eyes and some of the usual sparkle was gone. With a little good food and some rest she will be good as new again, Ida thought.

The year Penny was born, 1931, Ida and Tom Blair had become tenants on the farm neighboring the Harrisons'. They had come from Ashe County, North Carolina during the depression to find work. Ida had been the nurse who took care of Penny and her mother, Della, following childbirth.

She had kept in touch with Penny through letters and enjoyed hearing the news of Penny's sons, Bruce and Clifford, who were boys of nine and eleven when they left the farm. Nineteen years had passed and the boys were now married to two fine young women. They had always been Ida's "special children" as she once told the Harrison's. They were the children she never had. And, she had great respect and admiration for Penny.

"Any woman who can pick up the pieces of her life as Penny has done, needs all the help she can get." Ida told her husband, Tom, one day when they were discussing the young widow. Tom had agreed. "She's a survivor, Idy. Don't you worry about her. She'll get along jest fine!"

Penny had gotten along "jest fine" as Tom said. But it was not an easy matter. She was totally unprepared for Sam's death. The creed of the neighborhood was "neighbors help neighbors" and so when the call came for Sam to head over to the Lykens' farm that fateful evening, he wasted no time. It seemed there were some dead rats floating on the surface of the water in an old well near the barn and Jonas Lykens wanted them out of there. His hired man Jeb, was already harnessed up, he said, to be let down in the well to get 'em, but they sure could use an extry pair of hands.

Before Sam left the house, Penny gave him a fond kiss and hugged him through his sweaty shirt. "I love you, Sam," she said. "Hurry home."

"You better not wait up for me, Penny," Sam told her then. "I'll see you in the morning."

It was late in October, 1963, and the farmers in that area were putting the last of the corn 'silage into the silos for winter for feeding the cattle. In fact, Sam had just told her that was the last load of 'silage he had just run up into their silo. He could put the big machinery away tomorrow morning, he said.

But, at eight thirty that evening, the telephone jangled in her kitchen. She had been preparing an apple pie and her hands were covered with flour. Hurriedly grabbing a towel to wipe her hands, she rushed toward the phone. The phone rang four times before she could lift the receiver. It was their neighbor, Pete Holden.

"Hullo, Miz Carson?"

"Yes, Pete. What can I do for you?"

"Miz Carson, ma'am, your husband he… he… ain't…"

"Go on, Pete, what are you trying to tell me?" Penny asked, recognizing the panic in the man's voice.

"Could… could you come over here to the Lykens' place right quick?" was all she could make out of Pete's next sentence.

"Of course." Penny said, "I'll be there as soon as I can!"

Penny hung up the receiver, grabbed the keys to the station wagon and was soon on her way up the dusty lane to the Lykens' farm. If the boys had been home they could have helped her but they were out for the evening with friends and so she drove alone not knowing what she would find. Because she had her nurse's training and was a registered nurse, she was often called to a neighbor's house in an emergency, to dress a wound, or give an injection, and more than once to deliver a baby. She kept a bag packed in the station wagon with bandages, a stethoscope, a blood pressure apparatus, and other emergency items. She supposed this was just another call for the "neighborhood nurse".

In a few minutes Penny found that it was she who needed help. Her husband had tried heroically to save the boy who had toppled out of the harness used to lower him into the well and had fallen face down into the water. Sam had gone down to rescue the boy, Jeb, and had been overcome by some invisible force and he too ended up face down in the water of the old well.

By the time Penny drove up in the station wagon, rescue workers had come and with ropes and pulleys had pulled the men out of the well. Jeb's parents had already come and claimed his body and had departed in tears. One of the rescuers, a young man with dirt, perspiration, and tears on his face, ran to meet her, hoping to keep her away from the frightful scene but she would not be kept from seeing Sam. Nor could he keep her from performing CPR until she was exhausted and she was sure there was no hope of Sam's survival.

In time, she learned that it was not the drowning that had killed the boy first and then Sam. It had been silo gas that had permeated the soil and entered, through cracks in the stone wall, into the well. The gas had hovered above the surface of the water in an invisible layer of death. One could expect the deadly gas at the top of a silo but no one had ever thought that the gas could seep into a well.

For months Penny walked through a nightmare of grief. At times she thought that Sam must come walking through the kitchen door and hug her in the old familiar way. His last words to her, "See you in the morning," haunted her until Pastor Dave told her, "Think of it this way, Penny. Sam loved the Lord. He is in the place of Eternal morning. There's no night there. It's true; he will see you in the morning."

Because she could not bear to live on the farm without Sam, Penny sold the farm and moved to a little house on the West Shore of Harrisburg. The boys' school was within walking distance and they had a Christian coach for football.

To stay on the farm would have meant she would be sole owner of the farm and the herd of fifty Guernsey cows and young stock. She knew nothing of managing a farm. Sam had kept the books, and the records of their finances; she had been his help for anything he might need. They had a dream of the boys owning the farm someday. Perhaps they would start a steel construction business since steel buildings were popular with farmers and other business men. She would have time to write the books she knew were in her heart and they could go on a vacation to the shore once a year. That was their dream; now it was dust.

When Ida and Tom came to help her through the initial grief and the mammoth task of getting the farm and house and animals ready for sale, Ida asked, "Darlin', are you sure you want to move away from here? All your folks are here, and your friends. We all want to help if we can."

"Ida, I must stand on my own two feet. With the help of God I'll manage. I can't live here any longer. For one thing, I was never really close to Mother, as you know. When I was converted to Christ a few years ago, she didn't understand me. And Daddy didn't understand me either. Sam and I tried to explain that the Bible says we must be born again to be a Christian. They were insulted that we should even think they needed anything but faithful membership in Brighton Church. No, Ida, this is the time to leave and begin afresh. The boys and I will find a Bible Church and I'll stay close to the Lord. I'll survive. You'll see."

Survival had meant change. Ironically, the move was good therapy for Penny and the boys. The boys pitched in and helped with moving and settling into the little house. They liked the excitement of being close to a city and having a lawn and garden that did not take all their time and strength as the fields and stables of the farm had done.

Sometimes she could feel Sam's presence when she worked at unpacking their things in the new house. "I'll see you in the morning," he had said

"Okay, Sam, but in the meantime I have to make a life without you, and I don't like it. I'm angry that you left me with all this. I'm still young enough to enjoy your closeness and your arms around me and you're not here anymore." The tears would roll down her cheeks and the pain in her chest from the grief gripped her like a vise. She would stop and wait until the sobs subsided and then take up the task of making the house a home.

She had packed Sam's clothing and many of her own things and had given them to Goodwill. She couldn't let his clothes hang around to become a fetish. Sorting things was painful but it was also cathartic and eventually, the work was done.

In leaving the farm, she had taken one last look around the empty rooms, made sure the windows were secure, turned the key in the lock of the back door, and walked to the station wagon where the boys were waiting. She didn't cry. She was satisfied that she had done the very best she could at this time of her life and she was ready to begin another chapter in a different place.

CHAPTER FOUR

PENNY CARSON

Moving from the farm near Brighton had taken months of preparation. From late October 1963 until the first of May 1964 when the young family moved to the West Shore of Harrisburg, Pennsylvania, there was the day-to-day operation of a dairy farm. Milking fifty cows was a twice-daily task but with their "neighbor helping neighbor" philosophy and their regard for the Carson family and the tragedy that had happened to one of their own, the farmers worked out a plan whereby the cows would be milked twice daily, the stables cleaned, the plowing begun in early spring and the routine of farm life continued.

Penny, meanwhile, was busy not only with the packing and prep for the sale of the farm in April but also with writing and speaking before groups of rural families. As a nurse she had a unique opportunity to express her views and the need for more information about what had caused her husband's death and the death of the young man who had perished with him.

Her work absorbed her and helped to assuage her grief as she spoke before medical and paramedical groups about what could possibly prevent such tragedies in the future. She would begin her talks with the conversation she had with Jake Parker on the day following the accident.

Jake had been one of the rescue team but he was last to arrive on the scene. And he was too late to save the two men's lives. He had to assess the situation quickly. He sent someone for a simple house fan to help ventilate the enclosed space because he reasoned within himself that such sudden unconsciousness and death must have been caused by toxins near the surface of the water rather than drowning in the water. Once the fan was installed at the mouth of the well, the gas could be dissipated and the danger alleviated, he reasoned. That was what made it possible for the rescue team to recover the bodies of the two unfortunate men.

"If they would have known the gas was there and could kill them, they wouldn't have tried to go down there, no how!" Jake had told her as he stood with his hat in his hands in Penny's kitchen the next day. "If I had my way every rescue van would have a blower as part of their emergency equipment to do the same thing that fan did. And, I'm going to see that we have that here in Brighton."

So Penny recalled for her audiences the conversation, describing the efforts that the rescue team had made in bringing the men's bodies up out of the well. With a sturdy rope tied to his mid-section and fairly crushed by the weight of the men he brought up from the well, one by one, Jake had performed a sad and necessary feat that October evening before Penny arrived on the scene.

Penny's real purpose in describing the dramatic event was to inform and bring to the attention of rural communities the need to prevent such unnecessary deaths. The lethal danger of silo gasses became the solemn topic of interest around many kitchen tables in Brighton and vicinity. It was characteristic of Penny to expend herself and her energies to help others and she continued her work when she moved to the West Shore of Harrisburg in May, 1964.

CHAPTER FIVE

BATTLING COPPER AND LEAD

Nights were the most difficult times for Penny. Often, returning from a speaking engagement, she experienced insomnia but she had experienced insomnia and depression for years. Waking the next day she would sometimes be so depressed that she could not get out of bed. Six months following Sam's death she attributed her depression to that awful experience.

The year was 1973 and it was a decade since Sam's death and she saw no improvement in her sleeplessness or depression. She was growing thin and anxious and terrified that she was losing her mind. She obtained the name of a Christian psychologist and kept his card for weeks before she finally called to make an appointment with him.

Dr. Jack Foster had been studying the effects of nutrition and heavy metals on the human mind. His practice did not prevent him from flying to Florida from Pennsylvania every weekend to attend classes to prepare him to identify problems he had never considered before in treating his patients.

He enthusiastically applied what he had learned to treat those clients who were willing to try the nutritional approach to their healing. Penny wanted very much to be well so she wholeheartedly agreed to the plan Dr. Foster laid out for her.

First, Dr. Foster described his plan of action. A blood and hair analysis were to be performed at the Brain BioCenter in Princeton, New Jersey, where there was a laboratory that could ascertain the presence of heavy metals, such as lead and copper, in Penny's body. Then, upon receiving the results, he would be able to recommend a solution to her.

For the first time, Penny began to see a light at the end of the tunnel. She agreed to have the tests performed and drove alone to Princeton, New Jersey, from Harrisburg to stay close to the BioCenter for a few days.

In 1975, a few years after Penny met Dr. Foster, a brilliant psychologist named Dr. Carl C. Pfeiffer wrote a book entitled, "Mental and Elemental Nutrients" in which he described the effects of heavy metals on a human being's nervous system. His findings coincided with the findings of Sir Humphrey Osmond and Dr. Abram Hoffer of orthomolecular medicine and its benefits. Together, Dr. Foster and Penny read and re-read the writings of these pioneers in orthomolecular medicine.

Dr. Foster was very serious as he presented his course of action against the results of Penny's blood tests and hair analysis. "Penny, the copper and lead levels in your blood exceed the normal limits found in the average human being. So much so, that I am going to recommend a method of chelation that will take time but which will result in ridding your body of the heavy metals that I believe is the cause of your depression and insomnia, and the outbursts of anger we both realize are not typical of your behavior. Chelation is like using a lobster's claw to remove an obstruction. Zinc and manganese in megadoses will do that with those two heavy metals. They will chelate the metals from your blood stream."

"I'm willing to do whatever it takes to get well. I prayed for a long time that the Lord would heal me from these symptoms. If this is how He chooses to heal me, I'm all for it!"

"You'll have to try to hang in there, Penny. This will take a long time and your road will have dramatic ups and downs. At times it will seem like you are on a roller coaster, emotionally. If you will try not to be discouraged, I believe we will be successful in ridding you of these metals."

"I believe you, Dr. Foster. My question to you is this: where did the heavy metals come from? How did I get lead and copper into my body?"

"Both heavy metals probably came from the drinking water on your farm. Often, acid well water on a farm will leach copper out of pipes of brass or copper into the drinking water. If allowed to lay in the pipes overnight it will be drawn off in the first glass of water or cup of coffee and the person to be first up in the morning will receive a huge dose of poison. Did you have copper pipes in your farmhouse?"

"Yes, we did. We remodeled the farmhouse in the 1950s and had copper pipes installed. I was proud of the shiny copper pipes in my kitchen! But, I must say, we did have trouble with pinhole leaks after about five years. Big spots of moisture would appear on my kitchen ceiling from the bathroom above. I didn't know that copper could be leached into our drinking water!"

"If you were the first person to drink from the tap in your kitchen or bathroom, you got the full dose. Better to draw off the water for about five minutes before drinking it."

"I'm thinking of the people who bought our farm. They will have this problem too if I don't tell them what I've found."

"It would be a good idea to inform them. Also, you might include this as one of your lectures once we see if the results are really as I expect. We will know in a few months if this truly is the solution."

"So, I'm a guinea pig, am I?"

"In a sense, yes, you are. But I will monitor your progress carefully and document what I find. This will help others with symptoms like yours."

"In time you would have become a basket case!" Dr. Foster told her one day when her continuing good health was a source of excitement to them both. "Copper can kill you! Copper attaches itself to your nervous system like barnacles attach to a ship. It remains fixed there for years. Some people are affected mentally while others experience joint problems like crippling arthritis. If people only knew how much mental illness is caused by copper and lead, they wouldn't be satisfied until they got rid of heavy metals in their bodies and corrected the problem in their water supply."

Penny felt that she had been caught on the brink of a precipice and had been literally dragged to safety by the hand of God. "Suppose

I had stayed on the farm and had not decided to come here to the West Shore to live. I would not have met you. Years ago, my family doctor wanted to give me Ritalin but somehow I knew that was not the solution and refused to take it."

Dr. Foster continued, "Another source of lead in a person's body is paint. Today's paint contains a high level of lead. I hope someday a chemist will discover a paint that does not need lead to be effective. Today, though, lead can be carried into your body by sanding lead-containing enamel in preparation for applying lead-containing enamel! Until Dr. Pfeiffer, et al and their research, people thought nothing of working without masks or gloves and so lead easily accumulated in the blood stream of many industrious do-it-yourselfers!"

"You just described me, Dr. Foster! I prepped and painted all the woodwork in our farmhouse and often cleaned my hands of the enamel by using gasoline. I knew it was probably dangerous but I kept away from open flames and such. I thought that was the only danger to using those chemicals."

"I believe in the sovereignty of God. He surely spared you the dire consequences of lead poisoning and other dangerous chemicals as well. He doesn't change!"

"This was His answer to my prayer for healing all those years ago. When I was young and the boys were babies, I had such a struggle with my nerves and with anger. I thought God would never believe me if I said I was sorry because my temper would flare again and again and I would be in the depths of despondency."

"Of course, He heard your prayers!" Dr. Foster said.

"This whole matter of depression, anger, and sleeplessness was what brought me to the Lord in the first place. I wanted to be well before I accepted Jesus as my Lord and Savior, but He wanted me to come to Him just as I was. When I finally fell on my knees and said, 'I'll live for you this way without healing; all I want is You!' He came into my heart and filled me with joy and the assurance of my salvation!"

"But He didn't heal you miraculously at that moment, did He?" Dr. Foster asked kindly.

"No, but He gave me hope that I would be healed some day! I was healed, by faith, although healing was not instantaneous." Penny laughed. "I didn't think it would take twenty years and a hundred miles to get me well, though!"

"It took all that and the research of men like Dr. Carl C. Pfeiffer, Sir Humphrey Osmond and Dr. Abram Hoffer. If it had not been for men like them many people would still be hopelessly confined to mental hospitals."

"I must write about this and talk to people today, especially women!" Penny said as she left Dr. Foster's office.

Penny had a new resolve and a new purpose. The typewriter in her study rattled through the night as she wrote and rewrote her stories and articles for the newspapers. She worked and, as she promised, she stayed close to the Lord. Her conversations with Him in the dark times were precious, in spite of the ups and downs of the roller coaster ride she was on as zinc and manganese did their work. She cried out sometimes in her loneliness, and the Lord held her. Slowly the joy that had come to her occasionally in her grief and sickness stayed with her. She gradually recovered from the copper and lead poisoning. She began to move out of the shadows into the light of good health.

She laughed again… about little things. And she hiked on the Appalachian Trail with friends, swam, and played tennis, and rode bicycle. She was tanned and her thinness gave way to a softer silhouette. After more than a decade, she could talk about Sam's death without pain, and her chest no longer constricted in grief at the thought of him.

In the intervening years, Penny wrote to Ida about her illness and about Dr. Foster's help in her returning health. Ida took Penny's letters seriously and she and Tom investigated their own water supply and took heed to the warning about protecting against both lead and copper. They saw the difference in Penny's personality. Where she had once been tense and often troubled, the new Penny was exhibiting joy and a radiance they had not seen in her before. In their daily devotions, they praised the Lord for her recovery and for His warnings through her of the dangers that might be lurking on their own farm.

Ida had just said to Tom that morning that she thought that if Penny had not recovered from the chemical poisoning she would probably have sunk into a deep depression when her parents were both killed in the accident.

"I reckon you are right, Idy." Tom said. "The Lord works in unusual ways, don't He?"

"If we keep our eyes and ears open we can see his workings. I sure am thankful you believe as I do, Tom."

"I don't think I had a choice," Tom said then and winked good naturedly at his wife. "Believe me, Idy, I wouldn't have it any other way!"

Now, with Tom gone on an errand in his pick-up truck, Ida moved between the range, the table, and the refrigerator while she talked with Penny, her lunch guest, on the day of the memorial service for Aaron and Della Harrison, on a Friday afternoon in May, 1982.

CHAPTER SIX

PENNY'S WALK

"I told Tom to stay away this afternoon. He won't be here to tease you!" said Ida as she sat across from Penny at the kitchen table.

"But, I'll miss that, Ida!" Penny said, laughing. "Please tell him I am sorry he couldn't be here, too. You both have been so kind to me since the accident; I'll never forget your thoughtfulness. You know that, don't you?" For a moment tears stood in Penny's eyes. Ida couldn't bear to see her friend grieved, so she reached across the table and patted Penny's arm.

"Now let's jest set here for a minute and forget everything else for a little while. Things has a way of workin' out. The good Lord planned it so! He knows the end from the beginning and we don't. Besides, as I told Tom this mornin', it's a blessing your mother and father went together. One of them would have been lost without the other, had it happened any other way."

"Of course, Ida, you are right. In the past few days I have often praised God for His mercy. Dad always said he wanted to go quickly. Mother, too. But, as we all know, we simply can't choose such things."

"Here I am tellin' you to forget things and I jest stir everything up again with my chatter. Forgive me, Penny, I don't mean to cause you no more hurt."

Penny and Ida joined hands and bowed their heads as Ida asked God's blessing on their food. "Dear God, thank you for this food we are about to eat. May it nourish Penny and give her the strength she needs to carry on today. We ask these blessings in Jesus' precious name. Amen"

"Everything looks so good, Ida," said Penny as she admired the lunch Ida had prepared. A spinach salad with Penny's favorite Dijon mustard dressing was on the table, and cups of good rich chicken noodle soup were before them. Fresh baked dinner rolls hid beneath a napkin on the bread tray. Slices of strawberries and bananas were in dessert dishes at each place.

"I've been going strong since Wednesday when I drove down from Harrisburg for the funeral." Penny said. She had lived alone since her son Bruce married and moved to the neighboring town of Kendall where his brother Clifford and his wife lived. "Bruce and Cliff and their wives drove down separately yesterday morning in time for the funeral. It didn't seem necessary for everyone to come with me. Besides, as you know, I must stay in the farmhouse again tonight for the family meeting tomorrow. After four nights in the farmhouse it will be good to go back home. I plan to leave after Church on Sunday morning.

"Rob and Sara are staying with Sue and her children and Aunt Mitzi is staying there also. We can all have lunch at the farmhouse on Saturday before Mr. Banks, Mother and Daddy's attorney comes to read the will."

"Are you afraid to stay alone?"

"No, Ida, I'll be safe. There's my old room to stay in and with you and Tom nearby, I haven't anything to be afraid of! Sue asked me to stay with her, but I told her I needed to be alone at a time like this."

"Oh, I understand, Penny. It's just that if it was me, I'd have to lock all the doors and windows and then shudder in a corner somewhere 'til Tom would come home. That's the way I am."

"Ida, if you had been alone in your life as much as I have, you wouldn't mind, either. Thank God, you never had to know loneliness." Penny folded her napkin and laid it neatly beside her plate. She got up slowly from the table.

"Please excuse me now, my dear!" Penny smiled. "I want to walk in Locust Hill and calm myself before I have to meet all those people this evening at Pastor Dave's communion service at church."

"Good-bye, Penny. Come see us anytime. If Tom or I can be of help to you, you jest let us know. We'll be glad to do what we can!"

"I know, Ida. And thank you for your kindness and the good lunch. I'll be off now. You can watch me out your window while I take my walk to Locust Hill if it will make you feel better!" Penny smiled, and kissed the wrinkled cheek of her old friend as she opened the screen door and walked out onto the porch.

Ida waved to Penny as she disappeared around the corner. "May God bless and keep you, Penny," she murmured.

Penny had changed from her dark linen suit and heels to her favorite country clothes for her lunch with Ida. Her tailored white broadcloth shirt was open at the throat and the long sleeves were rolled up neatly to her elbows. Her faded denim skirt was belted snugly at her waist and on her feet she wore a pair of navy espadrilles that had seen better days. She knew the terrain she would walk that afternoon and was prepared for the marshy grass near the barn where the spring of water erupted, that she would encounter.

The bright afternoon sun warmed her bare forearms in a way she seldom felt in the city. She loved it. "Once a country girl; always a country girl!" she thought as she lifted her face to the western sun before she turned and disappeared from Ida's view around a clump of bushes.

CHAPTER SEVEN

THE MEMORIAL SERVICE

"**S**ue, I cannot imagine what your sister can mean! Leaving us all like this and running off somewhere!" Elderly Aunt Mildred Brooks, known as Aunt Mitzi to her nieces and nephews, addressed herself to a slender woman who was clearing the last fragments of food from the old-fashioned buffet in the dining room of the great farmhouse on the hill. The last of the memorial service guests had pulled away from the farm about 2:45 and Sue was eager to clear away the crumbs and get home to her girls who would be arriving from school in an hour.

"You know Penny tires easily these days, Aunt Mitzi. Ida asked her for lunch to make sure she rests at least for an hour today. The past few days have been a dreadful strain on all of us but I think Penny is feeling it most. After all, I can toss things off and laugh about them; Penny could never do that. The oldest daughter carries more responsibility than the youngest, you know. Besides, I like the food and the entertaining. That's my forte. Be glad I can entertain you, Auntie. Penny will be home before you know it!"

"While it is true that Penny is more serious about things, Sue, I must say, I could never understand her! To my way of thinking, she is much too aloof. But then, living alone all that time does take its toll. How long has it been since Sam died?" Aunt Mitzi had a poor memory and asked often about things which she had been told several times before.

"It was in the fall of 1963 and this is May, 1982; that is almost nineteen years ago, Auntie" Sue said, with a far-away look in her eyes, and very thoughtfully. She added, "Nineteen long years ago."

"Death certainly brings its problems, doesn't it?" Aunt Mitzi volunteered airily. "In this case, it might solve some!"

"Why, whatever do you mean?" Sue asked, aware of her aunt's sly manner but unable to believe she could be so rude that she could suggest the present grief could yield future joy.

"Certainly, my brother and his wife were quite 'well off'," Aunt Mitzi replied. "The farm must surely be worth thousands and these furnishings…" here she paused to touch a brass pendant on a drawer pull on the buffet, "…these furnishings! Quite a few are antique, I believe. Surely, these will bring a pretty sum!"

Quick tears came to Sue's eyes. She stood quietly looking at her aunt, unable for a moment to speak.

"Aunt Mitzi, please," Sue stammered. "I… I don't want to talk about such things now. There will be time for that."

"Sue, forgive me! I am too outspoken at times. I should not have been so rude. Your mother and father, my brother and sister-in-law, were never very fond of me. I knew it and felt very sad about it. To tell you the truth," Aunt Mitzi remarked with great dignity, "I have been embittered by their disregard of me. Sometimes it shows. You mustn't mind me! I say what I think. I do want to make things easier for you, Penny, and Rob."

Just then, the screen door in the kitchen slammed shut behind Rob Harrison. Darkly handsome in a light summer shirt and beige slacks, he carried baskets of flowers in each hand and deposited them on the floor beside his sister.

"Sue, you won't believe the flowers that have come this afternoon! I sure hope you and Aunt Mitzi can find a place for them all. Look at this!" He nodded toward the doorway through which they could see a deliveryman and his helper carrying still more fragrant bouquets up the steps. Aunt Mitzi hurried to the screen door with an antique iron dog as a door stop to keep it from slamming shut constantly. She bustled down the steps and across the lawn before Rob could catch up with her and they returned with still more flowers.

Sue arranged the flowers quickly, banking them under the windows in the dining room and living room until the house took on the appearance of a garden. She had never seen such an array of carnations, irises, daisies, roses, and hyacinths. Their perfume filled the air. Sue couldn't help but think with a bit of sadness that they were too late in arriving to lend their beauty to the memorial service just past.

As the deliveryman drove off, Sue, Rob, and Aunt Mitzi collapsed in the living room. Aunt Mitzi was seated on a sofa above which was a framed watercolor of the farm Rob had painted. Sue and Rob chose wing chairs in front of the fireplace.

"Aunt Mitzi, I'm glad you've come!" Rob stated, appreciatively, "I would have been at a loss to know how to handle the guests without you today. Penny wasn't strong enough to take all the turmoil and Sue has had her hands full taking care of all the food that keeps coming in from the neighbors!"

"I'm always glad to help, Rob. By the way, there was a man about your age who asked about you and Penny. He came in about noon. Penny had just left for lunch at Ida's and he came in and signed the guest register. Here," she handed Rob the book with rows of neat signatures of neighbors and friends who had called on them that day. "He said if I didn't mind, he would take a walk until you returned. I told him that would be about an hour. Here is his name!"

Aunt Mitzi pointed to a neat male scrawl. Rob carried the book to the window and in the bright light he read: J. Kent Hartman, and a Pittsburgh address.

"Hey! It's Kent Hartman! I haven't heard from him since the war. We were ASTRP cadets together at VMI." With a sudden burst of recollection, Rob turned to his sister. "Sue, you remember Kent, don't you? He came here to visit Mother and Dad when you were just a little kid." Turning to his aunt, he said, "You say he went for a walk?"

Aunt Mitzi looked confused. "Yes, he said so but I don't know whether he did or not! I'm afraid I interrupted Sue and him when he asked permission to walk on the land. There were some people wanting to meet Sue just then and I don't know where he went! I suppose he will come to the church service tonight, though. You'll get a chance to see him then."

Sue was anxious to go home to the children. She wanted to lock up the farmhouse and leave everything for a while. "Aunt Mitzi, hurry! We've got to go. You and Rob will have to go home first. I will follow you. Here's my house key. You might not need it since Sara is already there."

Aunt Mitzi followed Rob to the car. She was still wondering what had happened to the tall, handsome stranger with the curly gray hair she had interrupted in bringing some friends to Sue a few hours ago. She remembered his eyes behind the dark-rimmed spectacles. They were very direct brown eyes; and they had golden flecks in them.

It was four o'clock on Friday afternoon and the memorial service and the gathering at the farmhouse had ended about three enabling Sue to send Aunt Mitzi to her house with Rob to meet the girls coming home from school. Sara, Rob's wife, had stayed behind when everyone else in the family had entertained guests at the farmhouse. She and Rob could rest for a while before dressing for the evening. Sue felt the need for rest, too. Perhaps a shower and a change of clothing would refresh her, she reasoned.

Sue had locked the farmhouse door, knowing that Penny had a key in her pocket to unlock the house on her return from Ida's. As she drove away from the farmhouse, Sue had a moment of overwhelming sadness. Nothing would be the same again. The visits she had with her parents were ended abruptly. She knew that. Since she and Ralph, her husband, had divorced, their emotional support had meant more than anyone knew. How could she bear to return to this house and sort the things Mother and Dad had left?

The funny old-fashioned things she once despised were now priceless to her. There were the Larkin pieces Grandmother Harrison had earned as prizes for selling products from door-to-door in this community after the Great Depression took everything she had. There was a Larkin desk and a bedroom suite and an armoire. And there was the brown marble-topped wash stand and dresser in the guest room of the farmhouse. The headboard of the bed stood six feet tall and Grandmother Harrison's hand-sewn log cabin patterned quilt was spread as a coverlet on the soft mattress. Sue had loved to curl up on the bright colors through a rainy afternoon in summer when she was a little girl. And, there was the old spinet desk she knew Penny liked so much.

What would become of all the old familiar things? She thought about this as she drove up the road toward the village of Brighton. Surely, all the old folks in this village had to decide what to do with their houses and belongings. If not, their children had to.

She cared very much about these things. It was such a mammoth task to undertake with her children still at home and Ralph no help any more. Her employer at the nursing home in Clairmont would not allow her the time to spend on such a project and she needed the money she made as an aide to the nursing staff just to survive.

With finality, she said aloud, "Penny will have to come down and attend to these things. She doesn't have to work! She can do that!"

Beyond the village now and on the open road, Sue let the tears roll down her cheeks. As she drove, she cried. It is not safe for me to drive while I am so upset, she thought. But the tears she had fought back all day would not be held back any longer. She cried until her chest ached from the crying and then she cried some more.

Meanwhile, Rob and Aunt Mitzi had driven ahead and had unlocked and entered the little house where Sue and her two children lived. Sara, Rob's wife, who had remained behind to launder some things and write some letters was upstairs waiting for her husband. Rob was exhausted; he wanted to rest on the cool sheets.

A warm breeze stirred the dotted Swiss curtains as Sara turned back the covers. "Sara is still an attractive woman!" Rob thought as he watched her moving about the room.

"I'm pretty lucky," he said aloud to his wife.

"Why, for Heaven's sakes?" Sara asked as she brushed her short curls away from her forehead where the afternoon's heat had made them stick in damp ringlets.

"For one thing, I'm lucky to even have a mate. When I look at Sue I think about how hard it must be for her to keep this house and raise two girls without a husband. I realize how fortunate I am to have a wife who will 'hang in there' with me."

"Don't feel too sorry for Sue, Rob," Sara said, pettishly. "You know how your mother and father have protected her. They were very kind to her and the kids. And, I shouldn't wonder they passed a little money her way now and then."

"Well, if they did, I never knew about it. They had a rule that once a child of theirs grew up and left home, that was the end of it! I learned that a long time ago. Once I heard Dad tell Penny when we were kids and she asked him about his feelings toward us, he said, 'Don't come to me with your financial problems once you're married. When you marry, you're on your own!' And he meant it. For all I know not a cent ever left their hands to help any of us. Certainly no money went to us, or Penny, or Aunt Mitzi."

"I suppose it's the upbringing I've had, but I think that was a very unloving attitude. Sure, parents aren't supposed to give handouts all the time. However, it seems to me they could have helped Aunt Mitzi, at least. I'm glad we never needed their filthy, old money," Sara snapped as she folded some laundry, wrapped herself in a cool summer robe, and began to repair her nails by the window.

"That, my dear, is a miracle," Rob replied. "And as far as I know, it was a gift of God. Ever since I was a kid I could draw and such a talent doesn't grow on trees. Being an artist has supported us very well indeed. I was just lucky!"

The sound of a car on the gravel driveway below caused Sara to turn from her preoccupation with her nails. "It's Sue," she told her husband.

"Good!" Rob turned over and pulled the sheet over himself. He knew that his wife would wake him in time to dress for the evening communion service at Brighton. He knew, too, that Sue tired as she was, would not rest until she had set the table and put food out for everyone.

"Yep, I sure am lucky!" Rob thought as he drifted off to sleep.

CHAPTER EIGHT

THE MEETING

There were two ways to enter the meadow. One way led past the barn, through a marshy place, and along a pretty little stream that led to Locust Hill. Unknown to Penny, it was the direction Kent would take an hour after she left the house to have lunch with Ida.

Penny's path led away from the barn in the opposite direction. She headed westward and then south until she had arrived at Ida's friendly kitchen door. From there, the meadow was only a few yards away. In her childhood, Penny had often driven the brown-and-white Guernsey cows ahead of her along the path toward the barn to be milked. It was the cows who had made the paths through Locust Hill as they followed the same route day after day to and from the milking barn. In May, the cows could be found in the shade of the willow trees on the stream bank, contentedly chewing their cud with half-closed eyes.

Now, there were no cows in the meadow. The abundant pasture grass was going to waste this year. The fence needed repair; Penny could see that. Soon brambles would take over in Locust Hill. Locust trees were sparse on the hillside; they had once grown there in abundance.

It had been only two weeks ago that she had walked this path with her father. Although he was limited in how far he could walk with her because of his heart condition, he insisted it would do him good. Now he was gone. Sudden tears filled Penny's eyes as she thought of him.

Her father knew of Penny's love for violets and he knew where the richest patches of long-stemmed violets grew. They had brought bunches of them for Mother to fill the little milk-glass vase on the windowsill in the dining room. Now Mother, too, was gone.

The violets had dried in the vase because Mother had forgotten to water them. Penny had noticed them that morning and took a few to press between the pages of her Bible, in Psalms 23 where she read of God's comfort: "The Lord is my shepherd; I shall not want. He makes me lie down in green pastures; he leads me beside the still waters…"

Penny walked on the path as it curved around a high hill. She was deep in thought and soon she was out of sight of any houses or human beings. She was conscious of the stream where she and Rob played when they were children. The stream was off to the right of the path and ran along beneath a steep bank. To her left was a tangle of brambles and honeysuckle vines, now fragrant with white blossoms. She had entered Locust Hill. The path ahead was clear and except for a few branches she could easily lift out of her way, there were no obstacles.

It was hard to be gloomy on this afternoon in the sunshine. She felt her father's presence and it consoled her. She was satisfied that he had accepted Christ as his savior through Sam's efforts and it comforted her. She imagined him happy, without worry, without pain, and with the Lord. She was filled with a quiet joy.

Suddenly, overhead, a bright bird flashed against the sky and lifting her head, Penny could see a Baltimore oriole in the tallest tree. She heard its familiar song.

"Hey! Where's your nest these days, beautiful?" she called. "It looks like you've been up to your old tricks of trying to hide that hanging basket from me. I'll find it! But, don't worry! I'll keep your secret!" Penny smiled at the lovely distraction.

Spring and summer and autumn and winter; all the seasons in their turn would come to this valley whether she and her parents were here to watch them, or not. "Everything has its season!" She told herself softly as she pushed aside an encroaching vine.

Just where the path dipped down and up out of a gully very abruptly, Penny stopped to rest. She realized that she was very tired. A great white stone jutting out of the side of the hill looked like a good resting-place. She sat down, spreading her skirts over the rock with care.

A movement in the bushes ahead startled her and then she heard her name. "Penny?"

She lifted her head, surprised to hear her name called in this solitary place. Coming toward her down the narrow path was a tall man, carrying a coat over his arm, the sunlight glinting on his silver hair.

"Penny?" The tall man stopped in the path and stood very still for a moment before he spoke again. The pretty woman seated on the stone had turned her head toward the sound of the deep male voice, calling her name.

"Penny?" Again, the man spoke her name. Then, he added, "Kent Hartman!"

He took one step closer in the sunlight and shadow of the locust grove, uncertain that his words could be heard above the sound of the stream near-by.

"Kent!"

It was as if she had seen him yesterday, not thirty-five years ago. The voice was the same. No! It was deeper and more resonant, but Kent's voice nevertheless. He was tall. He had the muscular build and erect carriage of a military man. He had short curly hair that she remembered as dark brown. Now, it was silvery gray in the sunlight. His face and arms were tan. His teeth gleamed ivory-white against his healthy skin. He wore his white shirt-sleeves rolled up carefully and carried his coat and tie over one arm.

As she made one graceful move away from the stone to stand before him on the path, a pace away, she saw his eyes behind the dark-rimmed glasses and she knew that, indeed it was Kent. The eyes were brown with gold flecks in them. They were the same soft brown eyes with the disarming directness she remembered.

While she was looking intently at this surprise visitor, he was searching her face. For an instant, it was yesterday and she was young again. He saw her wide-open eyes with the dark fringe of lashes. The same dark eyebrows curved like quills over the expressive brown eyes, one arched more than the other, in surprise. He saw the olive skin, the white teeth between her parted lips.

He saw the faint shadow on her right cheek and knew the dimple was still there when she smiled. Surprisingly, there were only laugh lines by her eyes. Her hair was as silver as his own. It was short and curled softly across her forehead and framed her face. The small ears he remembered were hidden in the curls and in the ear lobes, barely visible, tiny pearls gleamed.

She was smaller than he remembered. Standing perhaps a bit under his chin if she were close to him; she was slender and dressed simply in a cotton shirt, open at the throat, the cuffs were turned back and the sleeves pushed up on her brown arms. The faded denim skirt had picked up Spanish needles from the brambles on the path. Her canvas navy espadrilles were coated with dust. She stood in front of him now with her feet firmly planted on the path. Her hands were in her pockets, grasping the house key. And she was very calm.

He remembered that her voice was soft. A thrill that began at the roots of his hair spread like wild-fire through his body. With control and caution, he remained silent and still before her.

"Kent! Welcome again to my parents' farm. It has been a long time since we have seen or heard from you!" Penny extended an unbelievably small hand. Her dark eyes never left the man's face. There was great sadness in them. As he took the small hand in both of his hands with their long, slender fingers, his eyes never left her face.

They stood for a long moment locked in this gaze that spanned the decades. For them, in that moment, the earth stood still and waited. Their eyes held them together as nothing else could do. Though no words were spoken, the past faded away and they were together. And they were alone in the wood-land with the Providence that had brought them there, with privacy only the Lord himself could provide.

Penny was the first to break the long silence.

"Since the only seat I can offer you is this stone," she said, with a little laugh, "Will you sit down and talk to me a while? Perhaps then you can tell me how you happen to be here in Locust Hill just as I am returning from my friend's house! And, what brings you here at all? Forgive me, but it has been so long since we have heard from you that

I am surprised. I can't think that you have come because of my parents' tragedy!"

Penny seated herself again on the white stone. Kent sat beside her. He laid his coat and tie on the grass and as he did so he saw there a clump of violets. He picked first one and then another until he had three to hand to Penny. "Do you remember that I like violets, Kent?" she asked simply. "Yes, Penny, I remember that you like them. This place brings back many memories to me."

Thinking that the conversation was already too provocative, Penny turned to Kent and asked, "Please tell me how you came to know about Mother and Daddy's deaths... that is what brought you to us, isn't it?"

Kent told her briefly of the rare business trip to Lancaster that had brought him to a hotel late in the evening with nothing to do but watch the local news broadcast. "When I heard your parents' names, I knew that I wanted to get in touch with you and Rob and Sue if at all possible. But I hesitated to do so because of the long period of time since I saw any of you."

"Be honest, Kent! You hesitated because of me, didn't you? You wanted to see me again. Am I right?" Her unexpected candor disarmed him.

"Yes, Penny, I did want to see you! I am a bachelor, having lost my wife about ten years ago. I have no right to impose myself on you and your husband. The last I heard from you was that you were dating your high school sweetheart and that you planned to marry when you completed your nurses' training. Because you are married, the prospect of seeing you; seeing you, that is, in the sense that we can have dinner together and reminisce, appears to be very remote."

Penny was very quiet for a moment and then she said, "I only wish I could tell you that Sam would be glad to welcome you to our house. If he were alive he would say, 'Come on over for coffee, Kent!' but that is not possible. You see, Sam was killed in a farm accident about nineteen years ago. I loved him very much, Kent!"

Penny didn't cry. Her expression was very sad as she added to somehow heal the awkwardness, "What is your story?"

Kent found it hard to talk. But he began to tell Penny about the death of his wife, a woman whom he found hard to forget and for whom there had been no one to compare. "I think you can understand from what you told me about Sam, how much I loved my wife. She was so close to me that I became like a hermit for a while, Penny. I have tried to pick up the pieces, but it has not been easy. I tend to throw myself into my work. That's why I'm on this business trip. I make trips that I would not have to just to fill the time. I'd go crazy if it weren't for my work."

"I'm like that, too. I think that someday I will have time to enjoy myself; but, not now!" Penny said wistfully.

Penny made a movement as if to get up from the stone, but Kent detained her. "Since we've had so little time today, Penny, and since we are both single again, may I call you? I must return to Pittsburgh tonight because I have a meeting in the morning that cannot be postponed. I am sorry I can't stay for the communion service tonight either, because my last plane leaves at seven o'clock from Harrisburg." "Penny," he repeated, "May I call you?"

Penny answered, "Of course you may, Kent. I will leave for my home in Harrisburg on Sunday night and will be home until Wednesday afternoon, the 19th. Then, I plan to take a much needed rest at the Cameron Mansion in Mt. Joy until Sunday morning, May 23."

Kent handed her two of his business cards. On one she wrote her phone number and address, as well as the phone number of the Cameron Mansion. She handed that card to Kent and tucked the other one into her skirt pocket along with her house key.

"I will look forward to our next meeting!" Penny said.

"And, so will I!"

Penny stood up and brushed the powdery dust from her skirt with one hand and held the three violets in the other. Kent stood up, too, and bent to pick up his coat and tie from the grass. He was reluctant to leave the grove, the stone, the stream, the flowers and especially, Penny. What had happened here had far surpassed his expectations. He had met Penny; he had talked with her and established his right to see her again; he had her address and phone number and she had his. In short, now he had all the information he needed to keep in touch with her, by the grace of God!

What was that verse Jeff quoted to him last night? "Trust in the Lord with all thine heart, and lean not to thine own understanding. In all thy ways acknowledge Him, and He will direct thy paths." He would have to look up the Bible verse when he got home, he thought. He wanted to remember it.

Kent replaced his coat and tie and ran his fingers through his hair quickly. He followed Penny up the narrow path toward the meadow. He sensed that Penny was in a hurry to get to the house. As they reached the meadow where there was no path but only meadow grass and daisies and marsh marigolds, he offered her his arm. She took his arm gratefully, for the ground was rough and uneven, and wet where the spring had erupted.

They walked on toward the barn and the farmhouse beyond, Kent retracing his steps for he had come this way to enter Locust Hill only a few hours before.

Up ahead, Bruce's station wagon was pulling into the driveway. The four young people had visited Pastor Dave and were detained longer than they had anticipated. In a few minutes, they alighted from the vehicle and stood waiting for Penny and Kent to make the short walk up the lane.

"I want you to meet my sons, Bruce and Clifford, Kent," Penny said breathlessly because the slight rise in the lane had taken her breath away as she walked. "And, this is Bruce's wife, Judy, and Clifford's wife, Ann."

When Kent had been introduced and the proper exchange of handshakes had taken place, Kent apologetically said, "I'm sorry to say that I must leave. I would like to stay and get better acquainted but, as I told your mother, I have a pretty tight schedule this evening!"

"Yes, sir," Bruce said. "We understand. Are you sure you know the way to Route 272? It's a straight shot north to Lancaster on that road. It takes about 45 minutes."

Kent assured him that he knew the way and Penny walked with Kent to his car. They exchanged their goodbyes and Kent drove away.

CHAPTER NINE

DINNER AT THE FARMHOUSE

As Kent's car disappeared up the road to the village of Brighton, Penny led the way up the porch steps to the dining room door of the farmhouse. She took the large iron key from her pocket and unlocked it, admitting her family into the house, fragrant now with flowers.

"Oh! My!" Penny exclaimed in surprise, "When I left this morning there weren't any floral arrangements. Now look! All of these from Mother and Daddy's friends and neighbors! Imagine how well-loved they were!"

"Yes, Mother," said Cliff, the younger of her two sons, "They were loved and respected. After all, I suppose that's really what life is all about. Since they have lived such a long life it is really super that they had so many friends."

"One would think they might have made some enemies, too," Cliff remarked, thinking how difficult the world was for him in his competitive business of steel construction.

Penny laughed softly, then, "They probably outlived all their enemies!"

"True!" said Cliff as he took off his jacket and put it over the back of a chair. With a few quick strides he made his way into the kitchen and in a moment he was absorbed in preparing sandwiches for everyone, believing they were all as hungry as he.

"Hold it on the food for me, Cliff. I'll wait for suppertime," Bruce checked his brother before he could prepare a sandwich for him. "I'm not hungry. All this has kinda upset me. I better pass." He went to find his wife, Judy, who had made a mad dash for the bathroom on the second floor as soon as they had entered the house.

Ann, Cliff's wife, was in the living room helping Penny as she straightened the furniture and prepared to leave the house in order. Perhaps someone will want to return to the house after the service tonight, she thought. The house must look presentable.

"Mother, don't you think you should rest for a short time!" Ann asked with concern in her voice. "You look tired and it will require a lot of standing tonight as you greet people at the church. Just talking with everyone will be exhausting."

Penny agreed and soon she had showered, shampooed her hair, and wrapped herself in a fluffy terry cloth robe. She seated herself before the dressing table mirror in her old bedroom.

She looked closely at her reflection in the mirror. Her olive skin had responded to the sun and there was a healthy glow on her face. Her forearms were brown where her white shirt sleeves had been rolled up for the walk in Locust Hill.

She shook her head and the damp ringlets fell, framing her face. She gave her silvery hair a final pat and was pleased with her reflection. She smiled at herself and her white teeth sparkled.

"Can it be that I have something to look forward to?" She asked her reflection as she recalled how Kent had shown interest in her this afternoon. She could not forget the long look they had exchanged in the grove. Thinking of that, the talk on the white stone, and the walk across the meadow, she wondered if it had been a dream. A sudden burst of delicious joy raced through her body and she got up and danced to the window where she had once stood as a young girl and looked down on the bare head of a young soldier who was obviously the roommate Rob had brought with him to celebrate the end of the war with Japan.

"Can a woman of my age know happiness again?" she wondered, hardly daring to believe it could happen to her.

Penny was stirred from her reverie by a knock on the bedroom door. Ann called, "Mother, are you ready for dinner? We don't want to be late for the service."

Penny's reply came quickly, "I'll be with you in a minute, Ann." She was putting the finishing touches to her makeup. Used sparingly, the cosmetics enhanced her natural beauty. The sun in the meadow had given her face a glow. Her lips only needed a touch of color and her eyelashes a bit of mascara.

She fastened a single strand of pearls around her neck. They fell within the neckline of a simple beige dress. Her beige pumps were stylish and gave her a bit of height. An approving backward glance in the full length mirror on the door and she was off down the stairs to dinner.

"Hey! Here she is," Cliff pulled a chair out and seated his mother at the head of the table. When she was seated, he turned to his brother and said, "Bruce, will you offer the blessing for our food, please?"

Bruce and Judy were on one side of the table and Cliff and Ann were seated on the other, with Penny at the head of the table as they each bowed their heads reverently. Bruce prayed, "Dear Heavenly Father, we bow our heads before Thee in thanks for this food and for the shelter of my grandparents' house on this evening when we think so lovingly of them. Thy Word is Truth, O Lord, and we praise you for it. Thy Word is our food and we are nourished by it in our spirits. In the precious name of Jesus Christ, I pray. Amen."

"Thank you, Bruce," said Penny. She was glad for her family and for the support they gave each other in this time of sadness.

As the meal progressed, the conversation was light and happy as they remembered the things that had happened that day. The two young couples had a pleasant visit with Pastor Dave that afternoon and they shared with Penny the conversation they had with him.

"Mother!" Cliff suddenly demanded, teasingly, "Who is this Kent person you introduced us to this afternoon and how did you get down in the meadow? I saw you walking across that marshy place. He took your arm. I saw that!"

Penny flushed and tried not to show her delight in the memory her son evoked. It was no use. They saw the pleasure on her face and laughed good-naturedly to ease her embarrassment.

With as few words as possible, Penny related her visit to Ida and her walk in Locust Hill on her way back to the farmhouse which coincided with a walk Kent was taking in the opposite direction. She told them that he was a friend of their Uncle Rob's who often visited the farm on their grandparents' invitation. She told them that she was a teenager at the time of the visits. He told her this afternoon that he had not forgotten her and wanted to see her again. He wanted to honor her parents also but was not sure he would be welcome after so many years.

She had assured him that he was welcome and she expected to see him again, socially, when it was convenient for them both.

"That's remarkable," said Ann. "That he should remember you and want to see you is like a premise for a romance novel!"

They would have proceeded with the conversation but they became suddenly aware that time was moving fast and they were expected in the church in Brighton within the hour. "We'll continue with the story another time!" said Penny. "Promise?" asked Cliff, who had opened the question that was on everyone's mind on both sides of the table, since they had met Kent at the farmhouse before he left for the airport and home.

"Promise!" Penny returned, laughingly.

"Mother," Bruce said, changing the subject, abruptly. "Judy and I and Cliff and Ann plan to stay another night here in the farmhouse so we can attend the family meeting with Grandma and Grandpa's attorney tomorrow."

"That makes me happy, Bruce," Penny said. "I need you all to be there."

At that moment, the phone rang. It was Ida and she was insistent. "You jest let Tom and me stay with you tonight, Penny!" Penny gave in to her friend's demand and with a laugh, she agreed. It was decided that the kind neighbors would stay in the guest room and that Ida would take care of preparing the meals on Saturday for the family since Attorney Banks was expected later in the afternoon.

Cliff was on his way upstairs when the phone rang again. He grabbed the phone and after a moment's pause, said, "It's for you, Mother."

Soon Penny was listening to Kent's voice. He wanted her to know that he would be in touch with her soon. "I must talk with you again!" he said, surprised at his own boldness.

"Wednesday morning at nine, then," Penny replied, with obvious pleasure. The young people could not miss seeing the flush of happiness that swept across Penny's face and grinned at each other with joy at the sight of it.

There were a few more sentences of conversation. Then, Kent said, "Good night, Penny. I'll be in touch!"

CHAPTER TEN

KENT'S FRIENDS

Kent had rented a car at the Harrisburg airport for this business trip into Lancaster County. He drove away from the farm in it and headed for Brighton only a mile away. At a familiar turn in the village road he passed the beautiful, stone, eighteenth century Brighton Church on his right. It was in the vestibule of that church he had seen Penny for the last time in 1947; until this afternoon. Thirty-five years had passed.

What did the future hold?

Driving north on Route 272 toward the city of Lancaster, Kent passed through little crossroad villages with strange names like The Buck, Truce, and Willow Street. Finally he arrived at the Host Hotel on Keller Avenue in Lancaster. It felt good to have a shower, shave, and to change into a fresh business suit, white shirt, and tie. He wrapped his muddy shoes from the walk across the marsh in newspaper and was glad he had packed a comfortable pair of loafers. He would meet Claudia in a few hours and it would be his last chance to freshen up before he met her at the airport. The plane was scheduled to leave for Pittsburgh at seven. With his luggage packed, he sat down and his eye fell upon a Gideon Bible on the night stand.

He opened the book to Proverbs and found the verse Jeff had given him last night. It was Proverbs 3:5, 6. When he had finished reading the verses, he reverently closed the book and reached for the phone. He wanted to call Jeff.

Kent dialed Jeff Cranston's number. The phone rang twice then Jeff's familiar voice answered, "Hello, Cranston's."

"Jeff. Kent."

"Kent, it's good to hear from you. How did things go today?"

"Great, Jeff! That's why I called. In a few minutes, I'm heading for Harrisburg. I want to thank you again for listening to me last night. I met Penny."

"You did? How did that work out?"

"She and I had a good private conversation and she agreed to let me see her next week. I think the Lord must have been doing some homework! At any rate, she is single also. If I hadn't followed my hunches, I would never have known that. I'll let you know about all this in a few weeks. In the meantime, I sure would appreciate your prayers for us, Jeff."

"Sure, I'll be in prayer for you both. Remember the Lord will show you the way, Kent. Just stay close to Him!"

"Yes. Good old Proverbs 3:5, 6! Good-bye, Jeff."

"Good-bye, Kent." There was a click at the other end of the line as the call ended. Kent set the receiver in its cradle. Then, he had a thought. He would call Penny before he hit the road. Some assistance from the operator soon put him on the line with her and after a few short sentences of conversation, he said, "I'll be in touch!" They said their good-byes and he hung up.

Suddenly, Kent felt young again. He picked up his luggage, checked out at the hotel desk, got in his car and headed west toward Harrisburg. He would have plenty of time to catch his plane to Pittsburgh.

As he drove through the beautiful but, to him, monotonous countryside, he determined to sort out his feelings. He was not accustomed to lying to himself; nor was he in the habit of denying his emotions. Emotions were extremely important to him. He was not, however, given to introspection. His work as a testing engineer in the early years of his career precluded that. He had been employed by a world-renowned builder of dams and bridges. He was now engaged in the lucrative business of constructing steel buildings. With his mind on such problems as stress-bearing walls and cargo-carrying loads, he seldom had time to spend thinking about himself.

The car sped along smoothly, and he relaxed behind the wheel. The sun was low in the west, sinking behind dark thunderheads. He wondered if there would be a storm. He was tired but happy, and happiness was a feeling he had not known for a long time.

Once, when he was a boy, his grandfather had told him never to look back. "Always look ahead!" He would remind Kent, frequently. And in most things the advice was good. Often in his professional career, he had reminded himself not to look back. A mistake made once need never be repeated. He learned from his mistakes as a young man, and had benefited from them, until now in his middle years, he found that other business professionals came to him for advice and counsel on major building projects.

When his frugal grandfather who had raised him died he left Kent with his mansion and millions of dollars. Kent carefully invested the money in various holdings, established an engineering consulting firm with offices in twenty countries and with his long-time partner, Todd Drake, named the company Hartman Drake Consulting.

In spite of his enormous wealth, Kent chose to make the contacts in Pennsylvania. It served him in two ways: first, he could keep in touch with people like Jeff Cranston in Lancaster County, men who had helped him get a start in the struggling years, men to whom he was grateful and for whom he had the greatest respect. And, second, it helped him to keep his wealth a secret from his friends. He chose to be among people. He liked people and to remain entombed in his office in a Pittsburgh skyscraper made him feel isolated and miserable.

On his desk at this moment were several contacts to be made. There were some consultations that would keep him out of the office for weeks. He regretted the time away from friends, particularly Claudia, but business was business and he loved the challenges!

Once, when his partner, Todd Drake, had ribbed him about his stoicism, Kent had thrown back his head and laughed. Todd left the room with his vodka in a state of some confusion and Kent followed him out on the terrace of Todd's fashionable townhouse. Beside the fountain, he had found Todd, staring into the water dappled by the stream that splashed into a basin from a concrete cherub's urn. It was Todd's wife's idea of romantic art and Todd hated it.

Kent, with his right foot resting on the curb surrounding the fountain, leaned his elbow on his bent right knee and said to his friend, "Drake, there is one idiosyncrasy of mine, you'll have to put up with, I'm afraid. I don't smoke or drink because I decided I must have a clear mind at all times. And with that stuff, I can't be sure my mind won't play tricks on me. There are too many people depending on my judgment. I can't risk a mistake caused by drinking hard stuff." He could have added, "Besides, I'm a Christian!" But Kent knew from experience that when Todd was provoked with him that would have angered him further, and alienated him even more from the Christ Kent served. And Kent desired to make his Lord attractive to Todd.

Drake had looked into Kent's eyes and saw that he meant what he said. He respected the guy, but he thought he must be nuts to refuse all the free drinks passed around these days. He said, "To each his own!" As he turned to go Kent detained him with a hand on his sleeve. "Just remember, Todd, although it's my choice to abstain from drinking and although I wish you felt the same way, for the sake of our friendship, I do understand your need to be one of the crowd!"

"One of the crowd?" Todd repeated. "You're right! I am one of the crowd. Socializing with people will always be important to me! The trouble with you, Hartman, is you don't care enough about socializing. Suit yourself. Your standards are too high for me!" Todd had turned and without looking back had walked across the patio and joined his friends inside.

That was the party at which Kent had been introduced to Claudia Brainard. She had overheard the conversation between Todd and Kent. She remembered that Kent was the abstainer. At her parties at least, to impress him, there was always a health bar of juices and milk.

But Claudia Brainard was not the subject of Kent's thoughts as he drove toward the airport. Nor were his business concerns on his mind now. Todd Drake, his partner in business, had returned from Madrid. Undoubtedly, there would be a report from him on his desk when he returned to Pittsburgh. Todd was more than capable of handling the business in Kent's absence.

He was thinking about the last few moments of his visit with Penny.

They had continued on their walk across the meadow toward the farmhouse. As they passed the barnyard gate, they saw a station wagon in the lane. A group of four young people were standing by the vehicle. They had just arrived and were wondering if anyone was around to let them in the door of the locked farmhouse.

"That's my son, Bruce, and his wife Judy, and my son Cliff and Ann, his wife. Come, let me introduce you to them!"

In a moment, by Penny's running to meet them and their running to meet her, the little group seemed to melt into a cluster of affectionate hugs and handshakes. Kent, standing respectfully aside, remembered looking at all the excited greetings. He was introduced. The looks of respect and welcome were genuine. He felt their amiable acceptance of him as their mother's friend.

Kent had apologized for being unable to stay longer. Penny gave him her hand for a moment, walked with him to his car, and waved to him as he maneuvered out of the driveway and onto the road that led to Brighton.

He tried to analyze the impact they had made upon him. The open acceptance amazed him; not only Penny's acceptance but her sons' and their wives' as well. It was incredible. The naivete and trust of these country people! Or was it the trust of a woman who loved God and who feared nothing?

"Could she believe that 'All things work together for good for those who love Him and are called according to his purposes'?" Kent wondered. He knew the verse was in St. Paul's letter to the Romans but he would have to look that up in the Bible when he got home.

There was only one person he knew who was like that and she was no longer living; Jeannine. Could Penny also have this quality? He would have to wait and see for himself if this was so.

He took a risk today. He returned to find his first love, and she had in no way disappointed him.

CHAPTER ELEVEN

CLAUDIA

Claudia Smith Brainard was standing impatiently tapping her foot. Her pose was that of a model trained to be decorous as well as decorative. Her thoughts were on several things at once. The delayed plane from Harrisburg had required a phone call to change the dinner reservations for herself and her escort for the evening, Mr. J. Kent Hartman. The concierge was informed that they would be detained for an hour and so, the dinner set for eight o'clock would have to be changed to nine. Would they mind a table in a less private spot? He asked. Yes, that will have to do, she had answered. And now as she glared out the plate glass window of Gate 39, she saw the lights of the plane as it set its wheels on the glistening runway and taxied to a stop.

Waiting. Always waiting. It seemed to Claudia that was what she did best. And waiting was not easy for her. What was important to her was the catch at the end of the line. Just like a fisherman waiting for evidence of a fish he would successfully land.

She knew that prostitutes were often called hookers so she didn't like the analogy when it was taken to its full extent but still it did fit her situation. She was not a woman of the night and she was proud of her own moral abstinent character, but she could see how such a person could be compared to a fisherman.

Once Claudia caught a man and reeled him in, the rest was easy. Sometimes she had to remove the hook from the mouth of an ineligible suitor and toss him back into the stream, his mouth sore and bleeding from the hook.

But, usually, her catch was excellent. With sportsmanlike tenacity, she sat on the bank of her life, casting out tempting bait. Sometimes, there was a nibble that caused her to give her full attention to landing her catch. Pulling hard, she had on occasion landed an eel, slippery and wiggling. The eels in her life had left her drained and disgusted. What she wanted was a fresh-water trout of a man. One she could savor and enjoy as she picked the bones and laid them side by side on a fine china plate.

Such a man was Kent Hartman. When Claudia had first met him at Althea's patio party she knew immediately that he was the fine catch she desired above any other. And she had begun a well-planned strategy to get his attention, or hook him, as the case might be! It often meant attending church services with him and taking communion whenever he did.

Just being introduced to Kent was not enough for Claudia. She had managed to get his office telephone number, his extension, and had been ingenious in tricking his private secretary, Marty, into letting her speak with him. That was the next day after the introduction. Never let it be said that Claudia Smith Brainard was not clever.

Besides that, she had succeeded in having several luncheon dates with him to discuss business, of course. And an occasional dinner date such as this one, now delayed, had been arranged from time to time.

Nevertheless, it had been most difficult to convince Kent to come to her apartment. Once when she thought she had him, he called to say he was sorry but he had a sudden call out of town and couldn't make her dinner party. Actually, she had planned to have another couple who also cancelled at the last minute, or so she said, and the evening was spent alone with a book instead of, as she had planned, alone with Kent.

A similar thing had happened just before Kent had left for this trip to Lancaster County. She had planned a surprise birthday party for Todd Drake's wife, Althea, in her apartment. It would be a cozy affair with everything very nutritious and healthful in deference to

Kent's taste. But that night she had come down with a terrible cold and had to call Todd at the last minute, and Kent, too. She spent the evening with "Dallas" on the mahogany-cased television set, with its nineteen inch screen, and a box of tissues. There she was, alone again, while Kent and Todd had taken Althea to an elegant restaurant to celebrate her birthday. The surprise had been hers, not Althea's!

Kent had left the next morning with a hasty phone call to tell her he would be out of town for five days. He refused to tell her where he would be staying in Lancaster. She asked him when he would be returning and he gave her the information from his US Air ticket and asked her to meet him at the airport on Friday night at eight. He said good-bye and left her listening to the hum in the telephone receiver when he hung up the phone.

It was not that he was impolite. And he was very generous in giving her the use of his brand-new Cadillac while he was gone. It was merely a set of circumstances that were no one's fault. But they were certainly discouraging. Claudia, however, determined to hang on doggedly, somewhat like the fisherman strapped to the prow of the boat who has hooked a marlin and will need all her strength to land him.

Learning of the hour delay in the plane's arrival did not serve to heighten her mood. But she made the call to the posh restaurant to postpone her reservation until the arrival of her partner. It would be at least nine o'clock until he would be with her at dinner.

The thunderstorm that had come up quickly blew over just as fast. It had been a noisy one with claps of thunder that seemed to shake the earth and there was lightning so bright that Kent could easily see his way to the airport terminal in spite of the power failure that thrust the lights in the car rental garage momentarily into darkness. He disposed of his car there and carried his luggage to the ticket counter, keeping his briefcase with him to put in the overhead. He intended to review the deal made with Whitcomb and McAllister in Lancaster. Their building would cover the area of two football fields on a plot of ground that had cost them a few million dollars.

He settled down to wait in the USAir terminal where some of the passengers were looking nervously at their newspapers and watches. Although Harrisburg International Airport was small and dingy, the waiting room was clean and cheerful. The time passed quickly and soon he would board the plane for Pittsburgh. It was a few minutes past eight o'clock.

While Claudia was waiting for the delayed flight to arrive, Kent was just boarding the plane in Harrisburg. He handed the stewardess his boarding pass, settled back in his seat in the non-smoking section, and fastened his seat belt. He was eager to return home. There were many things he wanted to attend to and the delay was a nuisance.

A young woman, with a leather camera strap over her shoulder and several books in her arms stood beside him in the aisle. She shoved her books in the overhead compartment, sat down in the aisle seat, settled back, and fastened her seat belt. She glanced at the handsome business man who was now seated beside her. She thought he looked like her father.

"Whew!" she exclaimed. "I sure didn't expect to be flying to Pittsburgh in the rain. This was a great day until that storm came up." She extended her hand to Kent. "My name is Carol Brant."

"I'm Kent Hartman, Carol. It's a pleasure to meet you."

The young woman had a rather large nose, bright blue eyes, and a fresh-looking complexion, with freckles on her cheeks. She wore a jaunty blue beret to keep her red hair in place. She was busy arranging her gear and managed to keep her precious camera in view at all times. She settled down with a magazine open on her knees but her attention wasn't on the printed page. Presently, she said, "I've had the most exciting day!"

"Oh? Do you want to talk about it?" Kent asked.

"Father told me not to talk with strangers on a plane since I was a little girl, but I can't help it. I might bore you, though. You see, I didn't do anything *very* special," she paused, looking at the neatly dressed man beside her. She assumed that he would know nothing of such a mundane thing as a country walk. "It was so lovely and different from what I'm accustomed to in the city. It was special to me... I took a country walk. Pennsylvania is beautiful in May. I took scads of pictures." With this, she patted the Pentax camera on her lap. "My boy friend gave me this last month for my birthday!"

Kent laughed. "Certainly that's special. You won't believe this but that's what I did today. I took a walk in the country, too."

"You didn't!" Carol was incredulous. This man she had met only a moment ago and who was obviously so sophisticated had shared in his way a simple pleasure with her. "A walk in the country by two such diverse people, in two different places… neat!" she thought.

Just then the stewardess began to explain the emergency equipment. Kent and Carol had fastened their seatbelts. The plane taxied down the runway and was soon aloft in the dark rainy sky over Harrisburg's West Shore. Kent, looking down over the wing of the aircraft wondered if he was passing over Penny's house. Where did she live? He felt in his shirt pocket for the card she had given him. 120 Simmons Place, Highland Park, he read. He returned the card to his pocket, thoughtfully. He used the farmhouse phone number an hour ago. He would use the Highland Park one… soon.

Kent and Carol released their seatbelts and sat back comfortably in their seats.

Carol began to talk about her day and her walk then and he listened. She had walked in Long Park in Lancaster and had fed the ducks on the lake. She had taken pictures of children at play on the swings and sliding board. She had watched young lovers walking arm in arm under the trees, among the well-kept flowers.

"I don't know why plane trips make me talkative." She said. "Nervousness, I guess."

"It makes the time pass quickly. If you had no one to talk with, it would be boring."

"I've told you about my walk, now, how about yours?" The knowledge that she would probably never see this man again made her bold.

"Okay. I will tell you about it," and Kent began to describe the farm, the meadow, and the grove of trees called Locust Hill.

"Neat!" Carol exclaimed, her large eyes wide. She swept her long red hair back over her shoulder and listened intently as Kent told of how he had followed a whim in returning to Brighton. He explained the tragedy that had occurred which had drawn his attention back to his wonderful farm experiences and the people who had welcomed him into their home when he was a young man. He wanted to pay his respects to the family so he decided to return to Brighton today for that purpose.

"It was thirty-five years since I last saw the place." He said. "But I must admit to you that I returned there for another reason."

"Care to tell me what that was?" Carol sensed this man was happy about what he had done that day and he was also glad he had run some sort of risk!

"I returned on the chance that I might see a woman who, when I last saw her, was about your age... about sixteen."

"You flatter me!" Carol laughed. "I'm twenty! But, go ahead! Did you see her?"

"Yes, I saw her," Kent said simply. He paused.

"Well?" Carol asked. It was as if she had known this man for years. Anyway, she had an English Comp 101 essay due in two weeks. This had great possibilities. Middle-aged love! Super!

"I am determined to see her again if she will see me."

"'If' she will see you!" Carol exclaimed. She threw back her head, her red hair flying. "People your age fall over themselves being polite, if you don't mind my saying so," she laughed good-naturedly. "But, I suppose that's how things were back when you were kids. Manners and everything, I mean!"

"Yes. We were taught by our parents to be respectful of each other..."

"And so you missed a lifetime with someone you really were in love with!" Carol added, audaciously.

"Perhaps I did. But I am sure if I asked Penny about it she would say that her years with her husband were precious because they loved each other, probably as much as Jeannine and I did. I have learned some important lessons through the experience of caring for my wife when she needed me most. Those experiences have made me a more compassionate person than I was thirty-five years ago, for sure!"

"If you're talking about maturity, I agree. Years of experience equal maturity." Carol drew an imaginary equation in the air with one long finger. "All I know is this: there aren't many people who would have the guts to go back and dig up the past like you've done." With a moment's reflection, she added. "Just suppose she had turned out to be an awful person... She wasn't, was she?" Carol had a look of mischief in her eyes as she asked Kent this question.

Kent's answer was not given immediately. He glanced out the window at the rain, and felt the tremble of the plane as its reverse jets slowed it for the landing. He fastened his seat belt securely; his young friend did the same. The wheels struck the runway at Pittsburgh airport. The plane sped up the slippery pavement to a smooth stop at the end of the tarmac nearest Gate 39.

Carol said, with a twinkle in her blue eyes, eager to know if there would be a pleasant ending to her composition on middle-aged love, "What did she look like, Mr. Hartman? Penny, I mean!"

Kent had unfastened his seatbelt and picked up his brief case. Rising from his seat, he answered her,

"She was more beautiful than I had remembered."

He helped Carol with her books and followed her out of the plane and up the ramp to collect their baggage. Carol turned to him and grinned. "Mr. Hartman," she said, "I sure wish you the very best!" She walked away, turned, and waved to him. Carol Brant in her blue beret with her red hair flying disappeared in the crowd of people waiting at Gate 39.

Beyond the vanishing, jean-clad figure of Carol Brant there was a bright splash of color which was moving rapidly in his direction. It was the glamorous Claudia in a bright red suit. She could not disguise from him the edge of impatience in her voice as she greeted him. "Just because it's the last flight of the day is no excuse for an hour's delay!" She complained unreasonably. She stood on tiptoe and kissed him on the cheek. "Hurry!" she said, "Let's get your bags and get out of here. Our dinner was set for nine. We are already late!"

CHAPTER TWELVE

DINNER FOR TWO

Claudia drove Kent's Cadillac to the airport to meet him but she took a taxi home. She had arrived at the airport anticipating a warm welcome from Kent; she arrived at her apartment a few hours later, chilled and angry. As she looked at her reflection in the mirror over the divan in her living room, she knew she had only herself to blame for what happened. It was her dumb luck with men again, she decided, as she reviewed the events of the evening.

It would have been great if she had not found it necessary to change the reservation from eight to nine. She and Kent were stuck there in the middle of La Seur's at a table so small she could scarcely keep from being nudged by the waiter as he passed by repeatedly with his trays of food and drink. It was no place for the intimate conversation she craved. What she wanted was a detailed account of Kent's business trip and what she got was so sketchy she refused to believe that was all he did.

Still, she thought as she sat across from this latest catch, he is by far the handsomest older man I have ever seen. In time he will realize he can trust me with anything. Anything at all!

His thoughts seemed far from her. She could not claim his attention. He was first occupied completely by the menu, then by a person at the table next to theirs; then, by the waiter returning for their order. It was not at all what she had expected. Other men had noticed her as she was seated at the table but to Kent she must be invisible for all the attention he paid her.

Kent had thanked her for meeting him at the airport. He had inquired about her health and the weather while he was gone, but he was obviously not interested in the intimacy she wanted. She excused herself and went to repair her make-up and when she returned their dinner was before them. Kent spoke very quietly and firmly as he caught and held Claudia's eyes. With a calm, cool, directness, he said very quietly, "Claudia, I'm tired of playing games!"

"Playing games, Kent? What do you mean?"

"I mean just what I said, 'I'm tired of playing games' with you. I have tried to discourage you in every way available to me without success. Now, I must be blunt with you, and I am sorry it has to be before dinner… there is never a good time for a conversation like this, it seems. Claudia, we cannot continue this… this friendship. I do not feel the same way about you as you obviously feel about me. It wouldn't be fair to either of us to continue."

Claudia stared into his eyes. Shocked at his statement, she choked on her first bite of food, grasped her napkin, and regained her composure, all without allowing her eyes to leave his for a second.

"Wha… wha… what do you mean?" she repeated her question and again he answered her quite clearly and distinctly.

"I am not in love with you, Claudia. You must have suspected that long ago. Furthermore, I cannot love you! Time has only served to confirm that and my separation from you this past week has further convinced me it is not wise to continue to see you. I believe you expect from me feelings I cannot have for you. I'm sorry."

Claudia gasped. She dropped her eyes to her glass of water. She raised the glass to her lips and took one sip before she suddenly realized what she wanted to do with all her heart. Without a moment's hesitation, she quite calmly threw the remainder of the water in her goblet across the table, extinguishing the candle in its center with an angry hiss, and drenching the man who sat, startled, across from her.

"You prude!" Claudia said, angrily. "I might have known you would be like this! I hate you!"

The dining room was suddenly quiet. The waiter quickly brought towels to help Kent mop the water from his face and shirt front. Before anyone could move, Claudia had grabbed her purse and fled by the street door where she hailed a cab and rode home in a rage. The cab driver asked appropriate questions and received appropriate, though angry answers, a hefty tip and an admonition to "Never trust anybody!" The cab driver, a woman, grinned and said she'd try to remember that.

At home at last, Claudia hurled herself on her divan without removing her expensive red linen suit and sobbed without restraint until she fell asleep, exhausted. In the morning, she revived and resolved to continue her life unabated. Within a few days, she made a hasty plan to leave Pittsburgh, fly to Bermuda, and take up residence there.

Kent, with one exception, heard nothing from her. The one exception was, when, a few months later, Marty, his secretary, shared a postcard she had received from Claudia. The postcard pictured a man in the prow of a yacht, strapped to his seat, pulling in his catch… a huge marlin! Her hastily scrawled message stated that she was on her honeymoon, that her new husband had told her the fishing was excellent, and she enjoyed the surf. She signed herself, Claudia van Dershon.

For a long moment, Kent had sat with the ice water dripping from his forehead, running down his cheeks and neck and saturating his shirt and tie. His hair was wet and at first he couldn't see. He removed his glasses and wiped them on his pocket handkerchief.

Surprise and anger quickly ran through his veins, but his good humor won out. He threw back his head, and laughed. Soon, couples nearby who had seen and heard everything began to laugh, too, at first nervously, and then, heartily, with him.

He gave the waiter a generous gratuity and left the restaurant by way of the men's room where he made some temporary and necessary repairs to his suit, combed his hair, and calmly walked out a liberated man.

Driving to his fashionable mansion in Pittsburgh's Mt. Lebanon, he began to sing. It was some foolish little song he used to sing in the shower when he felt good. It rolled out easily from his throat, deep and rich and terribly happy. He was free.

Kent's housekeeper, Mrs. Armstrong, had retired for the night, leaving a light on in the foyer. He looked into the mirror above the gleaming mahogany hall table. "What a day you've had, old boy!"

He rubbed his chin and adjusted his glasses. He had not liked to appear to be the "heavy" to the others in the restaurant. He was sorry that he had had to speak so plainly to Claudia, but he did not regret having done so. He grinned at his reflection.

"That dash of water," he mused, "It was like being baptized into a new life!"

He wanted to laugh again. He also wanted to call Penny and tell her what had happened. It was an immediate feeling that he wanted to share everything of importance with this woman he had just met again after thirty-five years.

In the morning at breakfast, he shared his adventure of the night before with his housekeeper. He knew she would wonder what happened to him since his expensive white shirt was damp and there was a blue stain on it from his wet tie.

"I don't think I can get that blue stain out of your shirt," Mrs. Armstrong said after the explanation.

Kent reassured her by saying she could dispose of it and Mrs. Armstrong replied that if he no longer wanted it she could make a little dress for her new granddaughter, the white linen being so fine, and all!

Kent laughed and told her she could certainly have the shirt! By the time Mrs. Armstrong returned with a tray of breakfast food to set before him, she already had plans for how to place the pattern pieces of the little dress on the parts of the linen shirt that had not been spoiled.

CHAPTER THIRTEEN

PENNY'S PRAYER

After dinner in the familiar dining room of her parents' farmhouse and the phone conversation in which Kent had said he would be in touch with her the following week, on Wednesday at nine in the morning, Penny went to her room and knelt by her bed. Her Bible lay open on the pillow beside her. She was deeply troubled. She read from the Scriptures the words of David in the 63rd Psalm: *"O God, you are my God, earnestly I will seek you; My soul thirsts for you, my body longs for you in a dry and weary land where there is no water. I have seen you in the sanctuary and beheld your power and your glory. Because your love is better than life, my lips will glorify you. I will praise you as long as I live, and in your name I will lift up my hands. My soul will be satisfied as with the richest of foods; with singing lips my mouth will praise you. On my bed I will remember you; I think of you through the watches of the night. Because you are my help, I sing in the shadow of your wings. My soul clings to you; your right hand upholds me."*

Humbly, Penny bowed her head before her Lord. She whispered to Him in the growing darkness of her childhood bedroom that without Him she could not live. "You, most precious Savior, are my Lord.

"In spite of the humanness of my joy, O Lord, I submit this matter into your hands. If this meeting with Kent is not of you, dear Lord, then I ask that you prevent me from continuing in this relationship. Without your blessing, Lord Jesus, I would be most miserable."

Pastor Dave's weekly Friday evening communion service would begin in half an hour. Penny dressed quickly, grabbed her purse from the bedside table, and hurried downstairs where her sons and their wives were waiting for her.

In a few moments they entered the Brighton Church Chapel quietly and took their places in a pew beside a stained glass window dedicated to a minister who had served Brighton Church for forty years, from 1835 to 1875, Rev. Lindley Rutter. The evening sun was just setting and the colors of stained glass fell upon the carpet in soft shades of red, green, and blue.

Pastor Dave Seymour entered the pulpit of the chapel by a side door that led from his study. He was dressed in a dark maroon robe with a white surplice. His dark good looks were crowned with a head of fine black hair. He had a pleasant face that was tanned by the sun because he delighted in the chapel garden flower beds and could often be found there weeding and watering the plants.

Tonight his brief sermon before serving communion to the congregants was taken from Romans the 8th chapter, the 28th verse: *"And we know that in all things God works for the good of those who love him, who have been called according to his purpose."*

By now, everyone in Brighton Church knew that the Apostle Paul was Pastor Dave's favorite Bible personage, outside of the Lord, of course. He delighted in speaking to them about what he called "Paul's Gospel", given to him by the Holy Spirit following St. Paul's conversion on the road to Damascus.

Before Pastor Dave had come to Brighton Church on being called by the congregation, former pastors had spoken often from the gospels of Matthew, Mark, Luke, and John. They had emphasized the importance of the Golden Rule and the Beatitudes. They had urged the people to follow the sayings of Jesus, and had adhered to the Gospel of the Kingdom.

By contrast, Pastor Dave's sermons often were taken from Paul's letters to Gentile congregations in the ancient world and they were filled with hope and encouragement to new believers in Jesus Christ.

Pastor Dave believed that through Paul's Gospel, people would come to behave as the Gospels taught but with sincerity borne of the Holy Spirit, not simply by human effort.

Pastor Dave's brief sermon on this evening declared the sovereignty of God in the lives of believers and his comforting words sank deep into Penny's heart.

Following his sermon, Pastor Dave prayed, commemorating the sacrifice of Jesus Christ on the cross of Calvary by drinking the cup and eating the bread that represented his holy body and his blood that was shed "for sinners for the redemption of our souls". And, he did not forget to recall to their minds Christ's resurrection from death and the grave because, as he said, "It is our belief in Jesus' resurrection that gives us power to live for our Lord Jesus Christ." He also reminded his people that Jesus was now seated at the right hand of God the Father in Heaven, there to welcome us in Glory.

Penny joined the others in the chapel as they passed by the two deacons holding the sacred elements of bread and wine at the communion table. On this night, communion was by intinction and Jonas Lykens and his wife, Anna, deacons of the church, served each person as they passed by them to return to their seats for the benediction. It was a reverent procession that left the chapel, following Pastor Dave's benediction, to walk out into the cool May twilight. It was a sacred silence. Penny need not have feared that people would surround her and exhaust her with questions she could not answer. This was a holy time indeed.

The following morning, Penny woke to a gentle tap on her bedroom door, and in a moment Ida appeared with a tray of food. There was orange juice and a poached egg with buttered toast, and a pot of Earl Grey tea.

"Do you know how precious you are to me, Ida? You were here when I was born, and you are here now when I need you. Thank you so much for all you have done and for taking care of the meals today for us."

"Well, when folks are hurtin' I'm needed. So I go. It does me good to see you get some rest. After all the excitement of this past week, you need it!"

"I had almost forgotten that I made arrangements several months ago to spend a few days next week at the Cameron Mansion as a sort of get-away, never realizing how much I would need it now!"

"So, on your way home to Harrisburg, you will stop off at Mt. Joy?"

"No, I'll go home first and make sure everything is okay there, open the mail and such. Then, I will go to the Cameron Mansion on Wednesday afternoon, the 19th. I will stay until Sunday, May 23. I will be home for a while before a Memorial Day cookout at my house with the boys and their wives. It will be nice to relax, and I need to prepare a talk to be given at a West Chester civic club meeting on the second Friday in June. That's just a month away!"

Penny took a bite of toast and it seemed to turn to dust in her mouth as she reflected on the events of yesterday. For a moment, the events of the evening before floated back to her. At first, the tears rolled down her cheeks, and then she shook uncontrollably as she leaned against Ida's offered shoulder.

"It's all over, Ida! My folks are gone. The house will be empty when we all leave by tomorrow afternoon. What will become of this place and all the things here?"

"Honey, it's like Pastor Dave said last night. He said, 'We will grieve because we miss our loved ones and that's right and proper to do. We have good memories and kind thoughts about them and in time the grief will pass.' Life goes on, Penny." Ida handed Penny a clean handkerchief from her apron pocket. "You're like Scarlett O'Hara, you never have a hanky when you need one!" Penny laughed shakily then, and soon returned to eating the breakfast Ida had brought.

As she sat on the bed beside Penny, Ida was thoughtful. Then she said, "Penny, who was the man you was walking with in the meadow yesterday afternoon? Tom said he saw you with a stranger as he was drivin' by. Now it ain't my business, but, then again it is, too! We feel like your guardian angels right now. I told Tom he was seein' things."

"No, Ida, Tom wasn't seeing things." As Penny spoke she set her cup of tea down on its saucer with a click that seemed loud in the quiet room.

"It was really an unusual thing that happened and I am glad to tell you about it. It may help me to understand it more clearly, as a matter of fact!"

"Well, if it's a long story, I better come back another time."

"No, it's not a long story but it does require some background or history as you call it. Tell you what! I've finished my breakfast. I will get a shower and dress and if you have some time then..." Ida interrupted with, "Sure. I can shell them peas for lunch that Tom brought in from the garden this morning while you tell me what's what! We can set out on the back porch a while." As she spoke she picked up the tray and hobbled down the backstairs.

Penny was up and out of bed by the time she heard the familiar click of the ancient iron latch on the door at the bottom of the winding back stairs. Within an hour she was seated on the wide banister that ran along the edge of the porch, shaded by the purple clematis that covered the trellis. Ida was seated in a rocking chair in front of her with her apron full of fresh peas that she was shelling into a metal pan that "pinged" with each pea that fell into it from her nimble fingers.

CHAPTER FOURTEEN

IDA RECALLS THE PAST

It was Saturday morning, May 15, 1982. In his home in Pittsburgh Kent was eating his breakfast, preparing for his company meeting in the city. The meeting had been set for a Saturday morning because many of the men were out of town during the week. They had agreed to sacrifice this Saturday morning from their own personal time, because of its importance to the corporation.

Meanwhile, Penny, almost three hundred miles away to the southeast, was singing happily in the shower. She was remembering the meeting in Locust Hill yesterday afternoon. The thought of seeing Kent again, of talking with him, of hearing his deep, male voice, of holding his arm as they walked across the meadow together, of having him confirm for her his intention of seeing her again soon, filled her with joy and made her heart sing.

Like a person once dead and now raised to new life, she felt at this moment that new blood was stirring in her veins. Certainly, hope that had once been dead was now revived. She sang praise to God by whose grace she was able to begin again, even after thirty-five years had passed since she and Kent had last seen each other.

"Lord Jesus," she breathed, "I love you for caring for me. Praise your holy name!" Then, solemnly, she said to this unseen but lovely Person, "I really do not know Kent. Thirty-five years can make a great difference in a person. And we were so young when we first met. But you know him, Lord. You know his heart. And you know my heart, too. You know that my feelings are those romantic feelings that make me want to sing and dance! Although I love to feel this way, I commit my feelings and emotions to you. I have one desire and that is to please you, Lord Jesus. So, if Kent is not a Christian, give me the wisdom and courage to say 'no!' to a relationship with him. In any case, lead on, Lord Jesus. I trust you with my life."

While Penny was thus occupied, Ida had settled herself in a rocking chair on the porch. She was shelling fresh peas from the garden. The task was so familiar to her that her thoughts were soon of Penny. "You were with me when I was born and you are with me now!" Penny had said this morning.

"Yes, indeed!" Ida thought. "I was with Della Harrison when the child was born in this very house; in the big bedroom to the southwest. It was surely a cold mornin' in February."

On that February morning, Ida was nurse for Della Harrison, who had delivered with great pain and difficulty, a baby girl. It had been a frank breech birth with the buttocks presenting first instead of the head as in normal deliveries. Dr. Bradford, perspiring and concerned, brought the baby forth from the mother. The baby girl was blue from lack of oxygen. Dr. Bradford reached for his suction and soon had her breathing. With a little slap on her buttocks, the child responded and was no longer blue. Soon the air in the bedroom was filled with the unmistakably new-born cry of Penelope Alicia Harrison as the doctor laid the pink bundle in Della's arms. "Thank you, Dr. Bradford," Della said weakly. She opened the blanket and looked at the now calm, pink little face peering back at her. "Are you going to be a good girl?" she asked, and smiled at her new daughter.

When he had delivered the afterbirth, Dr. Bradford clamped the umbilical cord with two hemostats in two places about two inches apart and cut the cord, tying it with a strong suture. He applied a soft bandage and Ida wrapped a wide flannel band around the infant's tummy to hold the dressing in place. After delivering the placenta, he removed his gloves and dropped them into a basin Ida held to receive them. He massaged the fundus of Della's uterus through Della's flannel nightgown to assure the bleeding was under control. Satisfied that all was going well with mother and baby, he reached for his coat that was hanging on the back of a chair.

Aaron appeared at the bedroom door and Dr. Bradford said, "You have a fine baby girl, Aaron; a good healthy one too! I've explained to Della that her milk supply won't come in right away but she should put the baby to the breast often to get her used to sucking. I will be here to check on Della and the baby tomorrow morning."

Ida helped the good doctor with his coat and muffler as he prepared to leave. They were downstairs by this time, standing at the dining room door. Ida had her hand on the doorknob ready to let the doctor out into the frosty air when he suddenly had an afterthought. He turned to the woman who had helped him with the delivery.

"Mrs. Blair, keep an eye out for post-partum depression. Della has not wanted another child. In fact, she was very angry when she came to me and found out she was pregnant. She was depressed, I think. Living here with very few conveniences can do that to a person. And, she has a very active little son. At any rate, the baby was not wanted. That may change once she sees what a precious little soul she is responsible for. Keep a watchful eye on her and let me know how things progress."

"Certainly, Dr. Bradford. Have a nice day, sir!" Ida cheerfully smiled and opened the door for him to walk out on the porch. He paused long enough to put on his hat and then proceeded down the steps to his Model T Ford and his waiting chauffeur. The car bumped roughly over the rutted lane on the way to Brighton where he was to see his next patient. In fact, he had three patients to see in Brighton before he could head for home.

A blast of cold air came in before Ida could close the door again. When she did she leaned against the door in exhaustion. She had had no sleep that night and it was doubtful whether she would get any rest that day.

Robbie was up and dressed and prancing through the chilly upstairs hall. Shouting at the top of his three year old lungs, he exclaimed, "Just what Robbie wanted... a baby sister!" over and over again until Aaron came out of the bedroom, grabbed him and carried him in to his mother and new baby sister. Robbie was not very impressed by this baby sister who was awful little and red. He wondered how he would ever play with someone that small. He put his thumb in his mouth and pondered the situation, gravely.

Robbie would need breakfast. So would Della and Aaron and she was hungry, too, so Ida busied herself in the kitchen and began to stir up pancake batter, fry bacon, and get the percolator going with fresh, hot coffee in the coffee pot on the back of the Columbia wood-burning stove.

Ida never forgot Dr. Bradford's words. She kept an eye out for any signs of neglect of the baby or depression in Della. Finding nothing to concern herself with during Della's confinement, she felt she had done her duty by the time she left the little family to go back to taking care of Tom. That was three weeks after the baby's birth.

Ida didn't take the command as from Dr. Bradford alone but from the good Lord with whom she had a close and loving relationship.

In time, what Dr. Bradford suggested proved true but it took great perception to discover it. The neglect Della practiced was subtle and could only be excused by saying that she was too busy to pay much attention to the little girl. After all, she had an active three year old son to watch and care for and he would demand his share of attention, to be sure. He would grow up to be highly intelligent and endowed with a talent for drawing that exceeded anyone's expectations. When he was a man, he said it was a "gift from God" that provided well for himself, his wife and their family.

Penny loved her big brother, sharing with him the few playthings she had. Given the opportunity to bully her, Rob did his best to take advantage of her trusting ways. Once when they were both dressed to visit their grandparents, Robbie lifted a rock and brought it down on his sister's head, sending her to the house to have the blood cleansed by an angry mother who took out her rage on Penny, asking her what she had done to provoke Robbie.

Ida was not a close friend of Della Harrison. In fact, she was only an acquaintance though they lived within a short distance of one another. Ida tried to establish a relationship with the woman and found it impossible. Della was always right. She was always in charge of things in the farmhouse and she had a strong desire to dominate. Della was a gossip, listening to her neighbor's conversations on the party line. Ida knew this because it had caused the first quarrel between them.

Ida had heard Penny's baby cries in the background while she talked through the receiver of her phone with another neighbor who had no children. Without letting her friend know why, Ida cut the conversation short and walked up to the Harrison house to confront Della with the problem, intending to ask her politely to not listen in on her telephone conversations, please. Della was so angry she slammed the door in Ida's face, refused to talk to her for a month, and never apologized for the habit which she continued to pursue until the day she died.

In time, Rob was elevated to a place of prominence because of what Della Harrison considered his superior knowledge and talent while Penny, in spite of her equally wonderful talent for writing became the scapegoat. Penny would write only until the age of ten when her increasing responsibilities on the farm would prevent her from having time or the privacy in which to create the stories that were in her heart.

Ida bristled whenever she saw the evidence of abuse Della heaped upon the little girl. "Why, do you know, Tom, she has that child ironing all the clothes for the family! All them sheets and pillowcases, shirts, dresses and aprons. My land, the child is only ten years old! What can that woman mean by robbing her of her playtime. I've half a mind to tell her a thing or two, but I daren't, Tom. It ain't none of my business. I aim to keep doing what I can for Penny. She's one of the Lord's precious ones, that little tyke!"

Doing what she could meant that Ida asked little Penny to her house to play in the cubby hole under the stairs with Ida's old dolls alone or with Ida's nieces, Francis and Louise when they came to visit. Outside, the lilac bushes that sheltered them from the sun soon became a lovely playhouse for the girls' hours of summer play.

Ida watched the child Penny carefully for signs of distress and tactfully did what she could to make childhood easier for her. Sometimes she sewed a little dress with panties to match. "The panties," Ida explained to three year old Penny, "Have a little button here in front so's you won't get them on backside foremost!" When she made the clothes, Ida always sent a note to Della to explain that she had some scraps left over from a sewing project. "I sure hope you don't mind, Mrs. Harrison. I couldn't let them pieces go to waste!" In reality, it was because Ida's heart broke when she saw the awful clothes Penny wore for "every day".

Ida saw in Penny the child she had longed for but lost in miscarriage. Never to have another baby, Ida grieved to see a lovely child like Penny abused and neglected under her very nose! It made her angry and she implored God to "Help that child to bear up under all that work. Lord, if it be thy will, take her out of that place and give her some happiness. She ain't never known love since she was born, Lord. Afore she dies, let her know love!"

Since she could not always be present with Penny, of course, Ida could only imagine what went on in the isolated farmhouse. If she had known about the dark closet in which Penny was shut against her will for punishment, or if she had heard Della just once call Penny "nothing", she would have begged Tom to let her go and rescue Penny immediately.

Ida became Penny's emotional parent since neither Aaron nor Della was able to express their love for her, if indeed they loved her at all. It was Ida who held Penny on her lap and read to her. It was Ida who listened to the Bible verses Penny memorized for Sunday School. It was Ida who greeted her with a hug and affectionate kisses and allowed Penny to hug her in return. Penny gladly did so. It was good to respond to the love of this kind motherly woman.

By the time Sue was born, Della had a schedule that she could handle with Penny's help. Penny often took Sue for rides in her carriage up and down the lane to Sue's delight. Sue developed crooked legs as an infant that became worse when she learned to stand and walk. She had to wear braces and a nurse visited her every month to take notes and to advise Della on how to care for her. Sue became the center of attention and it was not until Dr. Bradford suggested that Della give her a dose of cod liver oil each day that there was any improvement in the child's legs.

The Vitamin D in the cod liver oil was what Sue's bones needed and soon her legs were straight and strong. The only evidence of the braces was that there was a scar on each ankle where the cruel metal frame had caused pressure sores that went into the bone. Sue carried those scars all her life.

Surprisingly, Penny grew to accept her heavy responsibilities graciously. Sometimes she defended herself against the abuse and got put in the closet for being disrespectful. Her personality was all but crushed under the load Della and Aaron together placed on her thin shoulders.

Although it was a pretty picture to see Penny drive the cows to the barn for the evening milking, Ida, watching from her doorway with tears in her eyes, knew it would be hours before Penny would be able to go to her bedroom and read or lay down to sleep. And she knew the child had no time or desire to write.

It was Ida who had explained to Penny the mysteries of her own body and how to protect herself from the fearful (to Penny) flow of blood that threatened to stain her clothes. Ida had waited for Della to perform this most needed duty but Penny explained that "Mother sat on the bed beside me and cried. She didn't know what to tell me, Ida. And, I need to know!" Her complaint was born of need and urgency. Ida was angry that Penny was not instructed properly in the use of sanitary napkins. "Tom, that woman was too cheap to buy the child anything like that. I declare, I don't know what kind of person she is, and I don't want to know either!" She added emphatically.

Although it had been difficult to keep a respectful distance from the Harrisons' while secretly keeping "an eye out" for Penny, Ida had succeeded in nurturing and encouraging Penny from childhood, through adolescence, young womanhood, and now served as mentor during her widowhood. In many ways, Penny, always independent and self-sufficient, except for the Lord, had gone on ahead of Ida; Penny became the one to whom Ida turned for advice and comfort!

It had been Ida to whom Penny went one day to describe hesitantly but with a glowingly radiant face her personal experience with Jesus Christ. It was that experience during which Penny's will was broken. It was that experience that had settled once and for all time her assurance of salvation. In the quiet of her bedroom, she had knelt and given herself to the Lord Jesus Christ in the best way she knew how. The question of sin for Penny had not been difficult. She felt, rather, that she must be very sinful to bring such reproach and punishment from her parents. Common sense told her that she was not to blame that her parents whom she wanted to love in spite of their treatment had somehow missed the point and were merely church- attendees. They did not have a personal relationship with Jesus Christ.

Because of this revelation, Penny went to her parents to tell them the joyful news of her conversion and to beg them to find for themselves this peace and joy. But they would not. And consequently, though she would continue to live in close proximity to them for ten more years, frequently witnessing to them, it would be a long time before she would know how they believed. She was never to know the closeness with her parents that people who love the Lord know and call "fellowship".

After her conversion, Penny realized that it was the Holy Spirit who had cared for her during her difficult childhood. The Holy Spirit must have been there to protect her when she was afraid she would be harmed physically. He had comforted her in the orchard when she was a child of three or four on that day when she had run there crying to pick violets and Star of Bethlehem and in doing so, forget what had made her cry.

The Holy Spirit had been there with her when she had gone to the orchard with the little New Testament her Sunday School teacher, Mrs. Moss, had given her when she was six years old. Penny was determined to read the little book, beginning with the first words of the Gospel of St. Matthew. She never could pronounce the names of those who "begat" others, except where it read: "And Jacob begat Joseph the husband of Mary, of whom was born Jesus, who is called Christ." Someday, she thought, I will ask Mamma what the word "begat" means.

Penny became more and more convinced that it had been the Holy Spirit who had given her love for her parents even though they sometimes treated her badly. He never left her nor did he forsake her. Nor did he allow her to have more than she could bear. He convicted her of sin as she grew in her Christian life and it was he who was the comforter when she grieved over her pet kitty when she died. The Holy Spirit lifted her up and made her to walk in high places; he would not allow her to "dash her foot against a stone"; his wisdom fulfilled her need when her own wisdom was finite and flawed; he spoke, not of himself, but of Jesus Christ, the son of God. The Holy Spirit of God exalted the Christ, though he, himself, possessed the same attributes as God, the Son, and God, the Father. The Holy Spirit became for her the Paraclete, or Comforter, that Jesus promised his disciples would come when he had gone to the Father.

This same Holy Spirit indwelt Ida also. Patiently and carefully, Ida opened the Scriptures to Penny. While she read to her the words of Jesus, the inspiring words of the Apostle Paul and the comforting Psalms of David, Penny listened and learned until she could communicate with her Lord and study her Bible alone with only the Holy Spirit to guide her.

During one of the Bible studies with Ida, Penny discovered the Shulamite maid. Reading the Song of Solomon in the Scriptures, she thought that the young woman sounded like herself. The description fitted her. The Shulamite maid, although of Eastern birth and probably much darker than Penny, was indeed a lovely counterpart. She spoke of this to Ida and kept in her heart the thought that perhaps she might know what it was to be called "beloved" by a man someday.

King Solomon could not only love the Shulamite maid but he could also express his love in wonderful words of praise and adoration.

Ida told her that day that she thought it was entirely possible that God would bring this about in her life. She must trust Him to provide for her what was best, however. And with that Ida said no more on the subject. Penny was fourteen years old at the time. Much too young, Ida thought, to be concerned about such things!

CHAPTER FIFTEEN

PENNY REVEALS A SECRET FRIEND

Now, sitting on the back porch of the Harrison farmhouse with the unshelled peas filling the apron in her lap, Ida was stirred from her reverie by Penny who, in a simple summer dress and sandals, came through the open screen door to seat herself across from her friend in the coolness of the flowering vine's shade.

Penny had brought with her a piece of needlepoint on which she was working a floral design in soft shades of rose, blue, and lavender. The leaves were her favorite shade of soft moss green on a background of ivory. This would be the sixth seat cover she had worked in the same design. It would complete the set for her dining room chairs and would look soft and lovely by candlelight in her dining room at home.

As she worked on her needlepoint and Ida shelled the peas, the morning passed pleasantly. Penny sat on the wide ledge which formed the top of the railing that ran along the edge of the porch. Her cool summer dress of pale lavender caught the slightest breeze, its sleeves seemed to float in the warm air, fanning her and making a lovely picture for Ida to relate to Tom later that evening.

Although she was not the Shulamite maid, she was a beautiful woman, mature and radiant. Had the Shulamite maid grown to maturity she would surely have looked like Penny! Ida thought. It occurred to her that Penny had been given a gift. The Lord had given her the gift of a youthful appearance. With her firm skin and even white teeth, she had the beauty of a woman twenty years younger. Some would say it was the health habits she had; Ida would maintain that it was a gift of God.

On Sunday evening when the family, including Rob and Sara, Aunt Mitzi, and Sue, as well as Penny had left Brighton for their various homes, Ida would tell Tom about the conversation which now began with a question, "I don't mean to meddle in your affairs, Penny but... who was that man you was walkin' with in the meadow yesterday afternoon?"

Penny laid aside her needlepoint and, leaving the ledge where she had sat in the shade, took a rocking chair to sit beside Ida on the porch. As she had promised, Penny began to tell Ida about the events that led up to the strange man walking with her yesterday.

"When I left your house after lunch," Penny began, "I took the path through Locust Hill, as you know. As I walked through the grove of trees, I became tired and sat down on a stone to rest. I had just begun to catch my breath when I saw a man coming toward me. At first I thought it was Rob. But, then I saw the man had gray hair and when I heard his voice, saying my name, I knew it was not my brother. This man's voice was very deep and... I had heard that voice before.

"The man was Kent Hartman; a man I had not seen for thirty-five years. I must tell you that I was glad to see him but it was incongruous to meet a person I had not seen for such a long time in the meadow of my parents' farm. Actually, as it turns out it was quite natural that he should want to walk in Locust Hill again. He knew the path very well because we walked it often when he visited us here shortly after the war ended.

"You see, when Kent and Rob were only seventeen, they enlisted in the Army Specialized Training Reserve Program. In that program, they could study required military courses at a college until the age of eighteen and then they would be inducted into the regular army. For Rob that meant several months at Virginia Military Institute and then after his training, a long period of serving in the Philippines."

"I remember that. Tom used to help your Pa with tobacco harvest and combining wheat when Rob wasn't there to help no more."

"That's right, Ida, Daddy needed lots of help then. I was his 'hired hand' although I was only fourteen years old. I would get up at five thirty each morning to help milk our herd of nine cows before breakfast, bathe and dress and meet the school bus by seven thirty. You know I must have been hurrying to keep up with that schedule!"

"Yes, but where does this Kent Hartman come into the picture?" Ida asked with obvious interest.

"I'm coming to that, old dear. Rob arrived at VMI on August 4, 1945. He was there only ten days when World War II ended with Japan's surrender. In the short time since he began his studies on August 6, we received letters and cards from him and it sounded very exciting. He told us about his room-mate from Pittsburgh, Kent Hartman. And one morning unexpectedly, he called from Brighton to say he was on his way home for the weekend with his roommate, Kent!

"Well, in the time required for Rob and Kent to walk here from the village, we scurried around, preparing the guest room for Kent. I had already cleaned the guest room the day before and changed the linens on the bed so it was only a matter of swishing a dust cloth around the furniture to prepare it for our guest. Rob's room needed nothing; it was clean and neat.

"I changed into clean clothes while Mother finished preparing lunch. We would have a delicious meal after meeting Rob and Kent.

"I looked out the north window of my bedroom and watched them walking down the road. It was very dry and dusty and little puffs of dust rose up as they walked quickly toward the house. My heart beat fast as I looked down on the bare heads of my brother and his friend, Kent, who had removed their overseas caps and were standing there in the uniform of the US Army, talking and laughing with Mother and Daddy."

"It must have been a great sight, seeing Rob in his uniform, and all!"

"Oh, it was, Ida, but best of all, we were to have company, someone new to talk to; someone who would not look upon our work as commonplace, but as a new adventure. That is exactly how Kent reacted. Everything interested him. We took a walk through the corn fields and Daddy answered his questions about corn planting and harvest.

"As we walked through the tobacco field, he asked about that, too, and Daddy and I answered his questions. 'Where do you get the tobacco plants?' Kent asked. And Daddy explained how we planted our own tobacco seeds in long beds covered with muslin until the seedlings were large enough to stand without 'damping off or rotting'. One question brought on others until we were exhausted. It was stimulating and we enjoyed having someone show interest in us and the farm."

Penny went on, "Kent spent Saturday night with Rob in town and by Sunday afternoon, when it was time for them to board the bus for Virginia, we were sad to see them go.

"I was sure I would never see Kent again. After all, I was just a girl and he was a man of eighteen! But something happened within a week of his visit with Rob to our house.

"I had worked with Daddy in the hay field all that day in August and was very tired when I came in to the house that evening. I took a quick bath, ate my supper, and went to bed soon afterward. That night, I became very sick.

"I vomited. I became first very hot, and then so cold that my teeth chattered. At first, I had a very sharp pain in my right side. Finally, I became so sick I almost lost consciousness. I didn't want to disturb Mother and Daddy but they heard me and tried to make me comfortable. Hours later, after the cows were milked, Daddy came in for breakfast and it was then that he said we must call the doctor.

"Mother had bundled Sue into the car and we four headed for Dr. Bradford's office. Dr. Bradford examined me and told Daddy and Mother to take me to the hospital at once; the emergency room staff would be expecting us.

"I don't remember much after I lay down in the back seat of our 1946 Plymouth sedan. I don't remember how I got into the emergency room or how I got to a room where the nurses prepared me for surgery.

"The next morning I met Dr. Saul Pontius, my surgeon. He said, 'Pax vobiscum!' I knew just enough Latin to know that meant, Peace be with you!

"He told me that I had a ruptured appendix. He performed surgery and the offending appendix was gone but he had to put drains in my incision. That meant that I must stay in the hospital for several days so the nurses could dress the operation site. He told me that I was very fortunate to be alive. I was very grateful to Mother and Daddy for taking me to the hospital and for Dr. Pontius to see me and know what to do to help me.

"It was while I was in the hospital that I received the first of many letters from Kent. He must have realized what a close call I had and his first letter was sincere wishes for a complete recovery. After that, I looked forward to his letters that were friendly, brotherly, and funny; not at all suggestive or misleading. Kent was always a gentleman."

"It sounds to me like he fell in love with you!" Ida exclaimed in some surprise. In all her years of knowing Penny and her family, she had never heard this story. "Go on!" she said.

"I am sure now that it was Kent's love for me that kept him coming back to the farm for visits long after Rob had gone into the regular army and then overseas. As it happened, Kent was stationed in Maryland and could hitch rides to Pennsylvania for a weekend occasionally. He was closer to Pennsylvania than he had been while he was at VMI in Virginia. Of course he was happy about that.

"Now, I was not allowed to date local boys. Remember, I was just fourteen when I met Kent. The fact that he could stay weekends at our house angered Sam who was my high school boyfriend. He was jealous of Kent. I told him that Kent was a friend of our family and I felt that he was a brother to me. And, my parents did not say a word about discouraging Kent from visiting us. That was unusual, I know, but it is true. They enjoyed his visits and welcomed him until all of a sudden, when I was sixteen they changed their minds about it. They recognized the signs that we, as any young man or woman might, were in danger of falling in love."

"What did Sam think of all this? Did he know you cared about Kent by that time?"

"Oh, yes, he knew. And, I had a choice to make. If I encouraged Kent, I did not have any idea what my future would hold. With Sam, I knew he was faithful to me and that if we continued to date, eventually we would marry and live on his brother's farm; possibly, owning it someday.

"In the meantime, Kent continued to visit. We had fun with sledding and board games in the winter and with long walks in Locust Hill and the Hollow Road in summer. Sue and Aunt Mitzi often accompanied us and I was glad because they were our chaperones. I didn't want to lose Kent's friendship.

"If it had not been for Kent's letters and his visits during those lonely years, I would have been unable to cope with life. Mother was not the pleasantest person to live with. She was a strict taskmaster, requiring me to clean house, iron, and do many other chores beside the barn work Daddy needed me to do. I had very little time to myself and Kent's love for me and his encouragement and open admiration were soothing to my injured spirit."

"It sounds like the timing was not right for you two!" Ida said, thoughtfully. She got up from her chair, painfully, and went into the kitchen with her pan of shelled peas, returning in a few minutes with some iced tea for Penny and herself.

"Tell me," she said, then, "When was it that you saw Kent for the last time? You said he wrote to you but… when did you see him last?"

"It was Kent's way to ask permission to visit on any weekend furlough he had. So, in one of his letters to me he asked if he could visit and mother told me to write and tell him he could.

Two weeks later, a few days before he was to come, she changed her mind and said she did not want him to visit that Sunday. I was unable to phone him as I did not know his number, and I was sure a letter would not reach him in time. Mother said we should send a telegram, which we had never done before, and give him the message.

"We sent a simple telegram with the message that he was not to come. I was sorry that it had to be so blunt. I wanted him to visit but I wanted to be obedient to Mother.

"That Sunday morning Mother was not feeling well so she stayed home and Daddy, Sue, and I attended Church services. As I was waiting in the narthex in my choir robe prepared to walk to the choir loft with the rest of the choir members, a friend of mine, Mattie, whispered to me, 'Isn't that the soldier who visits your family sitting there?' and she pointed to the pew a few feet away from me where indeed Kent sat beside a stained glass window.

"'Yes, it is,' I said, and I went immediately to him. I said, 'Kent, didn't you get our telegram? I told you not to come today! But, it's alright! You are welcome to come home with Daddy and me and Sue after service.' I knew I could somehow explain to Mother how this had happened, later. I would have to face her disapproval and probably she would blame me for disobeying her. But, I would do anything to see Kent and visit with him since he had made the effort to travel to us.

"It was as if I had slapped him across the face because he had not received the telegram and had hitched rides from miles away in Maryland, looking forward to his visit with us on the farm.

"I walked with the choir members to the front of the church and sat in my seat in the choir loft beside Mattie. I looked down to the place where Kent had sat a few minutes before and he was gone! I tried to remain composed throughout the service but I was anxious to get home to Mother and tell her what had happened.

"When I related the events of the morning, she said, 'You could have brought him home with you, Penny! It would have been okay!' I guess I just stared at her in disbelief. I was confused and for days afterward was very depressed. I received letters from Kent thereafter but I never saw him again. I was in nurses' training when I received his letter telling me of his engagement to Jeannine. I sent a letter of congratulations; that was the last letter I sent to him and I received no reply."

"I reckon Sam was relieved," Ida said, wryly.

"Yes, he was. And, in many ways, to be honest, so was I. Now, I concentrated on my future with Sam and my nurses' training. Sam needed proof that I was loyal to him so he asked me for the packet of letters Kent had sent. We met one afternoon after school at the little park near the high school. I handed the packet of letters to him and he glanced through a few of them. I knew he would find nothing embarrassing or disrespectful in them because Kent and I had a pact between us that if ever other eyes saw our letters neither we nor the reader, would be ashamed. Kent respected me very much and had a great deal of self-respect.

"Within a few moments of reading the letters, Sam took some matches from his pocket and unceremoniously set fire to the letters, stirring the ashes so that all was consumed in the flames. He even doused the ashes with water from the thermos he carried in his lunch pail before he was satisfied that nothing would ignite when we left the park.

"Eventually, all the pleasant memories of Kent and our friendship took their rightful place in my subconscious mind where I've read that such things are known to reside. I was satisfied that Kent had found happiness with Jeannine because in the photo he sent me at the time of their engagement, they looked very happy. To see him happy was enough for me."

"So, he must have heard on the television news about your mother and father's deaths and decided to pay his respects after all these years had gone by?"

"Yes, Ida, and I was surprised that he chose to walk on the old familiar path in Locust Hill when he had the time and inclination to do so. If he had not, we would not have had the conversation that established his right to see me again. He took a great risk because he didn't know whether I was still married to Sam. His wife Jeannine had died ten years ago. Now he knows that I, too, am single and we can renew the friendship we laid aside years ago!"

"My, Penny, all this leaves me breathless! I suppose you will see him soon."

"When we arrived back at the farmhouse from our walk in Locust Hill, I had just enough time to introduce Kent to my sons and their wives, before he had to leave for Harrisburg for the flight to Pittsburgh where he now lives.

"He will call me at home this Wednesday at nine o'clock in the morning and we will make plans to meet sometime after that."

"There is more to all this, Ida. I have prayed that my Lord will lead me. I do not want to marry an unbeliever and that is a subject I have not broached with Kent. I am reserving any deep feelings until I know he is the one the Lord has chosen for me. Nothing is more important to me than that he is a believer in Jesus Christ as his personal Savior. Sam had that belief and I don't want to marry anyone unless he shares that most precious personal relationship with Jesus Christ."

"I can't tell you how happy I am for you, Penny! Come on, let's get these peas and dumplings ready for lunch, and fry some chicken, so's all of us can eat before Attorney Banks comes this afternoon."

Ida led the way into the kitchen where she and Penny were soon absorbed in preparing lunch.

CHAPTER SIXTEEN

IN PASTOR DAVE'S GARDEN

It was late afternoon before Attorney Banks concluded reading the Harrisons' will to their family. It was the initial phase, he explained, as there was much to be resolved before any monies could be handed to them as promised in their last will and testament. The farm, for instance, would need to be sold. That would take preparation and finalizing the details of such a transaction would be time-consuming. Each family member agreed that Penny should be the executrix as their parents had suggested. Attorney Banks would complete the necessary preliminary paperwork. He told Penny that he would soon be in touch with her.

The shadows were growing long when Attorney Banks got in his jeep and drove away from the farm and down the Hollow Road to his summer home at an old mill on Fishing Creek. He and his wife spent weekends at the mill beginning in late April; it was a restful retreat from his law office on East King Street in Lancaster.

When the meeting in the farmhouse broke up, Rob and Sara drove off in their station wagon with Aunt Mitzi whom they would drive to the railway station. She would board the train to Boston to visit friends. Bruce and Judy and Clifford and Ann drove off too in a hurry to return to their homes near Harrisburg. Sue returned to her little house to iron a dress for one of her girls for Sunday School at Brighton Church in the morning.

Ida and Tom were the last to leave. They made certain that Penny knew they would watch over the place when she left for Harrisburg after church in the morning. They had a key to the farmhouse.

As for Penny, she planned to stay one more night at the farmhouse. Early in the morning she would visit her parents' graves with flowers. After that, she would attend Sunday service in Brighton and then drive home to Harrisburg.

As she turned the key in the farmhouse lock this Saturday evening in May, she had a very important call to make. She wished to call on Pastor Dave and have the private conversation he had requested yesterday. He had told her to meet him about six o'clock in the Pastor's Garden situated behind Brighton Chapel.

She was a little early for their meeting and Pastor Dave had not had time to change his gardening clothes. He wore canvas gloves, an old, faded pair of denim overalls, and a chambray shirt with a hole in one of the sleeves, torn by the rose bushes this afternoon. He was removing weeds from the myrtle that covered the ground between the brick walkways and had a large basket beside him in which to discard them.

"Pastor Dave!" Penny called from the gate where she could see him intent on his work.

"Penny! Come in! Sorry you find me so shabby!"

"You look fine to me, Pastor Dave. You should see me when I garden. I wear the worst clothes I can find." Penny laughed easily and looked around at the birdbaths and feeders and the lush greenery everywhere. Peonies had begun to bloom and their huge pink globes filled the air with fragrance. The garden was still and peaceful.

Pastor Dave motioned to two benches that faced each other across the lawn under a shady elm. He sat in one while Penny settled herself in the other.

"Pastor," Penny began. "I go home to Harrisburg tomorrow afternoon after church services. Tom and Ida will look after things while I am gone. I will return next month to begin preparing the farmhouse for sale. Attorney Banks read the will to the family this afternoon. He told us it would be necessary to sell the farm in order to provide each of us with our share of the inheritance.

"You will receive a letter from Attorney Banks concerning the money they left Brighton Church. I think you will be pleased; they were very generous."

"Thank you, Penny!" Pastor Dave removed his canvas gloves and with a red bandana handkerchief he wiped the perspiration from his face. He laughed at his clumsiness. "I do apologize for my appearance; especially since it was I who asked you to come to see me this afternoon!"

"Please don't apologize! I like you the way you are!"

"I had a reason for asking you to see me this afternoon, Penny. I think you will find it good news. You see, last Sunday afternoon your mother had Aaron bring her to my office; she said she had something important to tell me. I thought that was very unusual but I agreed to see her after church service that day. She was very nervous and told me that something had bothered her for a long time. By the way, your father waited outside the office door. I thought that, too, was unusual.

"I'm not sure I should tell you this, but I will!"

"Please do, Pastor Dave. I want to know what happened."

"She told me that her conscience had bothered her for many years. She confessed that she had an unloving spirit which had made many people unhappy. She said she didn't know what to do about it. She asked me if God would forgive her. I said that he would of course. When she realized that, she broke down and cried.

"I explained the love that Jesus Christ had for her from the time she was conceived. I explained how God the Father had devised a plan from the beginning of creation to save all those who would confess their sins and come to him in repentance. She listened to every word I spoke. I told her that if she truly believed that Jesus Christ is God and would accept him as her Savior that her sins would be forgiven and she would be set free from their power over her. I told her also that Christ died on the cross, was buried and was resurrected for the sins of the world in general, but for her in particular. I asked her if she believed this and she said that she did.

"I told her that St. Paul wrote in I Corinthians 15:1-4 the entire gospel message for her and all of those who believe or will believe in Jesus Christ as Savior and Lord. He wrote: *Moreover, brethren, I declare unto you the gospel which I preached unto you, which also you received, and wherein you stand; by which also you are saved, if you keep in memory what I preached unto you, unless you have believed in vain. For I delivered unto you first of all that which I also received, how that Christ died for our sins according to the scriptures; and that he was buried, and that he rose again the third day according to the scriptures.*

"Penny, she got down on her knees; I know it must have been painful for her. She bowed her head and with tears running down her cheeks she did what I told her was necessary to become a child of God. She confessed her sins and asked the Lord Jesus Christ to save her from her sins. She stayed very still for a moment and when she rose from her knees there was a look of relief on her face that I had never seen there before. She had a sweet smile for me and I rejoiced with her that she had at last given herself to our Lord and had received his comfort and eventually, I told her, the assurance of her salvation would come to her, through the Holy Spirit.

"Whether that happened before her death the next day, I don't know, of course. What I do know was that she was contrite and repentant. I know our Lord heard her prayer and I wanted to tell you that your mother will meet you in Heaven!"

"Pastor Dave, you have made me very happy!"

"When I told her she should make a public confession of her faith before the congregation, she said she wasn't prepared to that yet. She said she had something to make right with you, Penny, before she could do that. Do you know what she meant?"

"Yes, Pastor, I do. When I was a child she was very abusive to me and I suffered very much because of it. Ida helped me to see that I must forgive my Mother and so I lived in a state of forgiveness, so to speak, because I loved her and wanted her to love me. The Lord gave me love for her that ignored the hurt! He has answered my prayers for my mother! Do you know what this means to me, Pastor Dave? I have prayed for her salvation all my life!"

"Penny, Your mother always attended church and was a good woman. I could not imagine she had never been saved."

"Pastor, she came so close to dying without Jesus Christ as her Savior. If she had died without Him, she would have spent eternity in Hell. I thank God she came to know Him in those final hours; if she had only told me."

"She said she would write to you. Perhaps there is a letter among her things at the house."

"Perhaps. I will look for it when I return. In any case, it is enough that you have told me this. I can't tell you how much it means to me."

"God's ways are beyond our understanding!" Pastor Dave said as he stood up and prepared to leave the garden. Come, Penny, I will have Mrs. Baker make us a pot of tea before you go!"

Penny followed Pastor Dave through the garden gate to her waiting car.

"Thank you, but no! I must go and attend to matters at the house. Thank you for all you have done, Pastor Dave!"

"Good-bye, Penny. God bless you!"

Pastor Dave watched until Penny's car disappeared down the road toward the village. He turned then, picked up the basket of weeds, and walked slowly to the parsonage through the gathering darkness.

CHAPTER SEVENTEEN

THE LETTER

At her desk in the bay window of the little house in Highland Park, Penny sat pondering exactly what to say to Kent. She had decided to write her thoughts in a letter that would be in Kent's hands before his nine o'clock Wednesday morning phone call to her. She hoped he would have time to think about the letter's contents before their conversation that day. It was very important to her that he understand clearly what she had to say. She began to write in her delicate handwriting on fine linen stationery.

Sunday, May 16, 1982, 6pm

Dear Kent,

I want to thank you for driving so far out of your way to see me when you heard of my parents' tragedy. I will always remember your kindness. It was good of you to come.

While I finished my last duties at the farmhouse before returning home, I thought about our talk on the white stone in Locust Hill. (How peaceful and lovely that place is!) I thought about you and me and the friendship that began again although thirty-five years had intervened since we saw each other last.

I have met friends at reunions and get-togethers, but I have never experienced the depth of feeling which accompanied our meeting. Perhaps it is because we were good friends, were always honest with each other, and have no regrets about our former relationship that I have gathered the courage to write to you about an important matter. It concerns my personal faith in Jesus Christ.

I am human, Kent, as you know! I am lonely, of course, because I am a widow. I am therefore very vulnerable and at the mercy of my emotions except for one very important fact: I am a Christian.

My love for the Lord is not out of a sense of keeping a law; far from it. I love Him because I want to love Him with all my heart and soul. It is a matter of the will, after all. No other relationship can ever be as important as my relationship with Jesus Christ. And I have learned to obey Him and remain close to Him out of adoration for Him who saved my soul!

I was converted several years after I married Sam. Quite by accident, I discovered the secret to a happy life. My Lord not only saved my soul for all eternity but He also healed me of something that could have snuffed out my life long before we could meet again. But that is a story I can relate to you some time in the future.

There was no time to discuss this matter on Friday afternoon in Locust Hill. I did not have time to ask you if you knew this Jesus as your Lord and Savior.

If you know Him, this letter will be received with great joy for we shall have established another common bond. If you do not know Him, this letter will be difficult, if not impossible, to understand and there can be no further contact between us.

I am adamant about this, Kent. If you have never been saved by the Lord Jesus Christ, I shall surely pray for your soul. But, if you know Him as your Savior and Lord, then, please tell me so that we may continue our friendship.

Sincerely,
Penny Carson

Kent read Penny's letter as he sat at the desk in his den. Through the window on that early Wednesday morning, he could see a row of peonies and clumps of well manicured azalea bushes in bright pinks along an immaculately groomed lawn. The sun was shining in the east window of the room, flooding it with light.

As he read, his heart leaped up within him until he felt as though his chest would burst with unspeakable joy.

"Praise God!" he whispered and then he shouted, "PRAISE GOD!" Again he shouted, "Praise God!" and laughed until the tears rolled down his cheeks. His housekeeper, Mrs. Armstrong, unaccustomed to such noise in the otherwise quiet house, came to the door.

"Are you all right, Mr. Hartman?" she asked, anxiously.

"'All right'? I should say I'm all right!" He exclaimed. "If all goes well, my search is ended!"

"Your 'search', sir?" Mrs. Armstrong asked.

"Yes! I will tell you about it later. If you will excuse me, I have a phone call to make!"

Mrs. Armstrong disappeared and returned with a silver tray on which there were a fine china cup and saucer and a silver urn of fresh-brewed coffee. Kent thanked her and she turned to leave the room, aware for the first time since she had known him of an obvious change in mood, from somber to ecstatic, in a matter of moments. She heard Kent say, "Hello, Penny!" and then she closed the door quietly and smiled to herself as she went down the steps to the kitchen.

"Kent! Hello!"

"I've just read your letter. I had to respond to you immediately!"

"Oh!"

"Yes! By your writing to give me your testimony for Jesus Christ, you have given me the opportunity to tell you that I know exactly what you mean!"

"You do?"

"Yes. Penny! I, too, am a Christian! I was converted when Jeannine and I were married and experiencing some difficulties. I can tell you about it sometime but for now, is it okay if I tell you I have had a similar concern about you?

"I have wanted to become involved with a Christian woman who would understand my love for the Lord Jesus Christ. I wanted to know about your faith and I was sure it would be one of the first things we would discuss. I have to tell you how elated I am that we both know Him!"

"Kent, I am happy, too! We will have a lot to share with each other!"

"When can I see you, Penny?"

"Well, I leave this afternoon for a self-imposed retreat to an inn in Mt. Joy where I often go to write and prepare my talks. I will return here on Sunday, the 23rd. Could you meet me there for dinner on Saturday evening?"

"Fine! But, how do I find this inn?"

Penny carefully explained the location of the Cameron Estate Inn in Mt. Joy, Lancaster County. Kent, realizing it was near a private air field he had often flown into, told her he would fly down on Saturday afternoon. Penny happily agreed to meet him for dinner in the inn's dining room at seven.

As she said "Good-bye!" and hung up, Penny was seized with a desire to cry and laugh all at once. Her joy was so great that she hurried to her bedroom and falling on her knees, exclaimed, "Praise God!"

CHAPTER EIGHTEEN

PENNY'S RETREAT

The Cameron Estate Inn in Mt. Joy, Lancaster County, Pennsylvania, stands beneath stately oak trees on a fifteen acre plot of ground near old Donegal Springs Church where the original Simon Cameron was a member. Early in 1700, the Cameron family came to America from Scotland and began to cultivate the fertile soil of Lancaster County.

In the next century, Simon Cameron's great grandson, Simon Cameron, became Abraham Lincoln's Secretary of War. Although the original Cameron family was poor, Simon Cameron had great wealth and bought the present Inn, making it his summer residence. That was in 1871. He was active in politics and is known as the father of the Republican Party in Pennsylvania. He not only owned what is now the Inn but he owned a mansion on Front Street in Harrisburg, now known as the John Harris Mansion.

Besides its obvious historical value, the Cameron Estate Inn, since October 1981, is well known for its hospitality and has been tastefully restored to the elegance of the Federal and Victorian periods.

Penny had discovered the Inn by accident and found it to be the perfect spot for concentration and relaxation. On this Wednesday afternoon in mid-May, she arrived at the gate and drove up the curving driveway to the Inn. She carried her luggage in the side door for she knew that there was no porter at this hour. She returned to her car, parking it in the upper parking lot.

As she walked down the gravel driveway to the Inn, she saw the young inn-keeper coming toward her.

"Catarina!"

"Penny!"

In a moment they were excitedly chattering about the beauty of the place and Caterina was talking happily about her latest project, an herb garden in the lower lawn. Because she had no luggage at the moment, Penny followed Caterina to where the lawn curved down to the stone wall that ended in a channel for a clear, swiftly running stream.

In the garden were heliotrope, hyssop, basil, marjoram, parsley and thyme, all marked with appropriate signs and very carefully protected with stones. The herb garden was close to the kitchen door where Andre now appeared to welcome Penny.

"How are you, Penny? We thought you would come in the winter!"

"No, Andre, I couldn't get away at Christmastime. You know how much snow we had and I am the one who keeps the sidewalks clear. I have been trying to get this lecture together since February. Coming here I can settle down and finish it in no time. It seems there are so many interruptions at home!"

"Catarina, before I forget to tell you, there will be a guest on Saturday at seven for dinner. Mr. Kent Hartman."

"Yes, I know. His secretary called and made the arrangements. We'll look for him!"

"The herb garden is wonderful, Catarina. I wish I could stay longer to walk around on the grounds. They are lovely. I have a lot to do. I hope my room is ready."

"Yes, it is. Do you want a pot of coffee?"

"No, thank you, Caterina. I would like a pitcher of water in my room, though."

Andre went for the pitcher of water while Caterina helped to carry the bags. Penny carried her typewriter and a box of supplies. Caterina was obviously delighted to see Penny and wanted to know if the publisher had accepted her latest manuscript.

Penny was pleased to say that after several resubmissions, it had been accepted and she was relieved that most of the work was completed on the new book.

Penny had only one full day to devote to her writing at the desk in the dormer window of her third floor room. She determined to use her time wisely so that she could spend a day shopping in Lancaster for a dress that she could wear to the Saturday night dinner with Kent in the Inn dining room.

Friday morning, Penny found herself in Ladies' Better Dresses at Watt and Shand's, the department store where Della had taken Penny to buy clothing since she was a little girl. Nostalgia swept over Penny as she recognized some of the sales people. Many of them remembered Della Harrison and expressed their sincere regrets to hear of her death. It gratified Penny to know that they remembered her mother so well. Aunt Mitzi bought her clothing here also. She thought that if it didn't come from Watt and Shand's, it was not of the best quality.

Of the four dresses the clerk brought to the fitting room for her to try, Penny chose a lovely rich purple dress that fitted her perfectly. The clerk admired the beauty of the woman who wore the dress. The color enhanced Penny's lovely tan skin and was a perfect foil for her silvery gray hair. "It looks like the dress was made for you!" She exclaimed. "I like it!" Penny said, and she followed the clerk to the counter where the dress was packed carefully among white tissue paper in a large box. As Penny paid the clerk she smiled happily. "Thank you so much for your help!" she said, and hurried toward the escalator with her purchase.

Friday afternoon was spent in having lunch at the Rendezvous and then a trip to Shaub's Shoe Store in Lancaster to choose a pair of shoes and handbag to complement her new dress. Feeling very rich and extremely blessed, Penny headed back to the Inn where she spent the remainder of the day engrossed in her writing at the desk in the dormer window.

To prepare for Saturday evening, Penny took her Bible and walked out among the trees in the garden. The silence there was lovely and the atmosphere brought her close to her Creator. "Well, here I am, Lord!" she breathed. "I am yours to lead and direct on this most wonderful day when I will see Kent. I know You are blessing us and I want with all my heart to receive what You have for me. I yield my will to You, most precious Lord. Please lead me in my devotions this afternoon."

On the day Kent had given her the three violets, Penny had placed them in one of her favorite chapters in all of scripture and she turned to that place now.

It was I Chronicles 4:10. It was the prayer of a man named Jabez. Penny began to read aloud as she sat on a rustic bench beside the little stream at the foot of the garden walk: *"And Jabez called on the God of Israel saying, 'Oh that Thou wouldst bless me indeed, and enlarge my coast, and that Thine hand might be with me, and that Thou wouldst keep me from evil, that it might not grieve me!'* And God granted him that which he requested."

"Lord, Mother bore me with sorrow just as Jabez' mother bore him. I might have been named Jabez for the same reason because my birth was so painful to her. His name means, "I bore him with sorrow", as your Word says! No matter, Lord, this is my prayer today: that You would pour out Your blessing on Kent who has been searching diligently for Your will in his life. If I am to be a part of Your will for his life allow us both to know that so that we may praise You for Your loving kindness to us as Your children. In Jesus' precious name I pray, Amen."

Penny sat for a short time listening to the peaceful sounds of the stream and then she got up and carrying her Bible up to her room on the third floor of the Inn, she put aside her sweater and shoes and lay across her bed, closed her eyes, and was soon fast asleep.

At four o'clock Penny woke to the sounds of new Inn residents being admitted next door. She glanced at her bedside clock and realizing it was soon time to prepare for Kent's arrival, she slipped out of bed, put on her slippers, and went to the closet where she had hung the royal purple dress. She laid her things out on the bed and went into the bathroom to prepare her bath.

Soon, the Shulamite maid was sitting in fragrant bubbles that surrounded her; she felt the luxuriant warmth of the water as it drew all her anxieties away, leaving her relaxed and feeling rested as she stepped out on the bath mat and dried herself with the softness of a pure white towel. Dressing in a pale pink silk dressing gown, she seated herself at the vanity and surveyed in the mirror the happy face of a woman in love.

CHAPTER NINETEEN

AT THE INN

"Gracious Lord, I praise You today for Your Creation and for Your power and glory. But especially for Your caring and Your love for me who am Your child. I love You, Lord Jesus, and wish to please You in all that I do and say.

"This afternoon, as I kneel before You here in this lovely place, I am conscious of a great change You are bringing about in my life and I don't want to spoil what You have in store for me. Ever since Jeannine was my wife and since her death, I have wanted a woman who knows and loves You as I do. I know from Your Word that being unequally yoked with an unbeliever is not Your will and I have been searching for the woman whose love for You is genuine and true. Otherwise, our relationship would be a disaster. You have shown me the consequences of unequal yoking and I see that it is not Your will for me.

"As I look forward to meeting the woman I trust is the right mate for me in this phase of my life, I need Your guidance. I am a man, prone to judge from outward appearances, which in Penny's case is truly sensational. But, keep me from falling for the physical Penny and help me to fall in love with the spiritual Penny who loves You as her Lord and Savior.

"Lord Jesus, please keep me from spoiling the sanctity of our relationship. I want to withhold that part of me that wishes to be instantly gratified. I want to consummate our love for each other in the marriage bed and not before. I need You, Lord, for restraint and patience through your Holy Spirit as I wait for the day Penny and I can be one.

"Grant me wisdom and a good sense of humor to carry us both through the period of time between our engagement and our marriage night. I want to be the intimate partner Penny deserves. I ask that You will grant me the manly approach to loving my mate.

"Lord Jesus, please bless this woman I wish to make my wife. If it is not her desire, may I be able to graciously accept her decision. Her happiness is paramount to my own. I love Penny, Lord, and I trust our conversation tonight to You and to Your keeping.

"Thank you for Your love for both Penny and me and for how You have led us by various paths to the one that has brought us together in these past few weeks. In Your precious and holy name I pray, Lord Jesus. Amen."

Kent got up from his knees as he had knelt by the bed in the room in Cameron Estate Inn. The room was called the "Dutch Country Room" and his secretary, Marty, had selected it for him. It was located on the second floor of the inn and was a spacious bedroom furnished with a king-sized bed and a private bath. There was a magnificent needlepoint tapestry on the wall and the fire was already lit in the huge fireplace. From the window there was a view of Donegal Creek and the woods beyond.

Kent stood at the window and was transported in his thoughts to the morning's activities that had brought him to this place. From the flight in his private Cessna 340 from Pittsburgh to Lancaster Airport to the cab ride to Mt. Joy and the Cameron Estate Inn, all had been without incident. Even putting his plane in a hangar overnight was no problem to the personnel at the Lancaster Airport and he was confident that he would be able to leave in the morning to return to his home by noon on Monday, May 24. This much he knew; he must have time with Penny tonight. It was the most important plan of the day.

Dinner with Penny was scheduled for 7 so he glanced at his watch and saw that he had time for a brief nap. He lay down on the soft counterpane and was soon sound asleep. Before he fell asleep he was conscious of the opening and closing of a door in the hallway and of footsteps softly climbing the stairs to the third floor.

By 6:45, Kent was seated at a round table in a private alcove by a window in the dining room of the inn. He could see whomever entered the dining room and kept his eye on any new arrivals. At last he looked up and saw Penny enter and inquire something of the hostess who took her in the direction of his table. He rose and pulled the chair out for Penny and greeted her with a hug. His lips grazed her soft silver hair as he moved her chair closer to the table. "It's good to see you, Penny!" he said then. "I didn't think you would be here so soon," Penny answered him.

"I've been here since about noon. I have my own plane so I arranged to fly to Lancaster Airport." Kent answered. "I'm staying overnight. I will return to Pittsburgh tomorrow morning."

"Oh!"

"I know it's a surprise to you but I want to have a conversation with you that is completely private and I could not see that happening if the only private space was this dining room and the living room beyond where everyone congregates after dinner."

"You are full of surprises, Kent!" Penny laughed. "But, you are in control of things and I like that about you."

The waiter arrived with the menus and left them to choose after he received their drink orders of Perrier for two. In a few minutes he returned and they ordered the Chicken Cordon Bleu with salads. The presentation of this simple dish was as elegant as Andre could design and Penny appreciated it. "Lovely!" she said.

Kent could not keep his eyes from Penny's beautiful appearance. Her deep purple dress was regal and set off her dark complexion and silver hair to perfection. He tried to concentrate on his food and found it impossible. "Penny, you are gorgeous!"

"So are you!" She laughed to think of a man as 'gorgeous' and he caught the message. Their eyes met and melted together as they had done in Locust Hill that afternoon. The whole world disappeared in an instant and they were in a place of their own choosing.

"Did you have a good flight this morning?" Penny asked to break the silence and bring them both down to earth.

"Yes! It was very uneventful. And the personnel at the Lancaster Airport could not have been more cordial and helpful. I can fly out tomorrow morning at nine without any trouble, they told me."

"When did you learn to fly?" Penny asked.

"My grandfather wanted me to fly before I could drive a car! I learned on his plane and then once I could buy my own, I purchased this Cessna. I am very pleased with its performance."

"Tell me about your grandfather, Kent."

"My grandfather Conrad Bristol was my maternal grandfather who raised me from the age of eleven. I lost my parents to divorce when I was very young and I don't remember much about them. My grandfather was my guardian and he loved me very much. He was disappointed in my mother and tried to make up for her neglect by his devotion to me; he brought me up properly!

"That's why he wanted me to be a part of the ASTR Program and join the Army when I was eighteen. He knew that I needed to experience the discipline of the military life since he was a military man. Grandfather Bristol was a graduate of West Point."

"Grandfather died several years ago. He left me a large amount of money which he put in trust until I was twenty-one years old; then, I benefited from his generosity and started my own engineering consulting company."

As the two friends ate their dinner, Kent told Penny of his past experience in engineering, of learning from his mistakes, and of not looking back, as his grandfather had told him, but of looking forward, always.

"He sounds like a wonderful person!"

"He was, Penny! I could not have asked for a better mentor. One of the best things he taught me was to forgive my parents for their neglect of me when I was a little boy. When I met my parents as a teenager I could speak to them without being angry and I tried to understand them. I was taught to respect my parents."

"It is hard to understand why parents sometimes do not love their own children. One would think that was a given; but it is not. Many children have to come to terms with that while they are still quite small."

"It's a hard lesson to learn, Penny; but it isn't fatal. We can rise above such things; especially, if we have given our lives to the Lord."

"How did Jesus become your Lord, Kent?"

"It is a long story but in its essence, the Lord came to Jeannine and me at about the same time. We wanted children very much and after many miscarriages and danger to Jeannine's health, we were advised by the physicians to give up having children of our own. It was devastating to both Jeannine and to me."

"It did not happen immediately, of course, but one night we knelt together and prayed that the Lord would give us peace about the matter and come into our lives and take control from that moment onward. We confessed our sins of selfishness and pride and He forgave us and from that moment He indwelt us both through his Holy Spirit and opened a whole new life for us."

"Jeannine and I dedicated our lives to helping the impoverished children in our neighborhood and the Lord gave us love for them that we would never have known otherwise."

The waiter came to remove their empty plates and returned with their order of Key Lime pie drizzled with raspberry sauce for both. Fresh coffee followed in a moment and Penny exclaimed again at the beautiful presentation. It was a dinner to enjoy completely.

"The Lord comes to us at the point of our deepest need, doesn't He?" Penny began. "At least, He did for me. I had wanted healing from depression and prayed often for healing but without success. Then, one day I knelt and asked Jesus to come into my heart; without healing me, if that was His will. And He forgave my sins and came to live in me through his Holy Spirit just as He did for you and Jeannine. By the way, He healed me; but it took twenty years to realize that miracle!"

"You do not know how excited I was to read your letter and find that you were born again! A great burden lifted from my shoulders and hope returned to me. For years, I had been searching for a woman who loved the Lord as I have come to do!"

Sometimes the Holy Spirit makes us break out in goose bumps of joy and this was one of those moments for Penny. "Oh, my!" she said, happily.

"Do you suppose we can finish here in a few minutes and go to my room to talk?" Kent asked. "Don't worry! We'll keep the door open so no one will suspect us of being indiscreet; though we might want to be!" And he laughed heartily.

CHAPTER TWENTY

A PRIVATE CONVERSATION

With their delicious dinner over, Kent led the way to the veranda and together he and Penny walked down the steps to the lawn. He took her to the stream where the moonlight was playing on the water and where it cast long shadows on the grass. There was the sound of laughter from the dining room. A waltz was playing on the stereo in the living room where people were gathered around a table playing cards; others were dancing.

The air was cool and damp. Penny shivered and Kent took off his jacket and placed it around her shoulders. He drew Penny close to him as he did so. Gently, he kissed her cheek and then released her and, grasping her arm, he led her back to the house.

"We must stir up the fire in my room. You will have pneumonia if we stay out here!"

When they had climbed the stairs to the second floor and proceeded to the north end of the corridor, Penny laughed. "My room is just beyond that door and up a flight of steps!" She indicated a doorway to her right that led up to the room known as "The Loft" to the Inn staff.

"How convenient!" Kent laughed, too, at the thought that Penny would be sleeping in the room above him during the night.

"Somehow, that's comforting," Penny said.

"When we've had our conversation, I will see you to the door, but not up the stairs, Penny, although I would like to do that. I respect you, and I don't want to cause any embarrassment to you by seeming too familiar!"

"That's fine with me!" Penny said with a smile.

Soon Penny was seated by the fire in Kent's room where the door remained open to allay the suspicions of any guest who might wander past the room. The warmth of the fire began to creep into her bones and warm her. She turned toward Kent with a grateful expression on her lovely face.

"Kent, thank you for your concern for me; I am not accustomed to being waited on, I can assure you!"

"If I have my way about things, all that will change soon. I have a purpose in meeting you here. I want to spend some time talking about our future; my future and yours."

Penny was aware of a sudden change of command. No longer feeling independent and totally alone, she sensed in herself a great relief. She felt like leaning on this strong man. She felt like letting go of the decisions and burdens she had carried so long and allow Kent to help her carry them. What was this change she felt? Was it weakness? No. Was it laziness? Heavens, No! Was this the unmistakable moment when a woman knows intuitively that she is in the presence of the man with whom she wants to share her life?

Aware that Kent was speaking, Penny made an effort to bring her mind back to the room at the Inn. She consciously turned her attention to his words and his expressions. She would take out those feelings later and examine them in the stark light of day. She must keep her feet on the ground and not allow herself any romantic feelings. She must be realistic. She must remain detached. She must wait for him to reveal himself to her. In time she would be better able to judge what kind of person this man, Kent Hartman, really was.

Kent had reached down to pick up another log for the fire. He put it carefully on the flames and stepped back to survey the sparks that rose up the chimney. The log slowly caught fire from the glowing logs beneath it and the flames leaped up brightly.

Kent came and sat down on the velvet wing chair opposite the beautiful woman. "Penny," he began, "I know that this is early in our relationship. I realize that you have had a great shock in the deaths of your parents and the full impact of that has not even yet affected you.

It may suddenly hit you one of these days when you least expect it. But I know also that time is an essential element and I feel that I must express my interest in you now while I can.

"You see, Penny, I want you to be my wife and share my future, whatever that may hold. I must return to my home tomorrow morning before you are awake. I don't need your answer immediately but I do want you to know that I am in love with you and I can promise you a comfortable life with me."

Penny, who had been listening in wide-eyed concentration to this man who was now seated across from her, remained silent for a moment. When she spoke she chose her words carefully and thoughtfully and without emotion. She remained seated in the velvet chair with her head resting on the softness of the cushioned backrest. Her hands rested on the arms of the chair. There was no motion in her hands. No nervousness or self-consciousness; no vanity or self-conceit in her voice as she answered Kent with intelligence and tenderness.

"I would be a fool if I did not recognize in your attention to me at my parents' home and here at this lovely place, a certain concern and caring for me. After all the years we have been apart to have you return at the time I most needed you seems almost like a dream. Even now I have to shake myself to make sure I am awake. I have had to deal in reality so long, Kent, that I am not accustomed to lovely things like this happening to me. Not that reality can't be lovely. It's just that, for me, reality has meant hard work, many tears, loneliness, grief, and pain for years and years. Would I feel home-sick for that life even though a life of comfort is what I think I would be happiest in? I really don't know."

"It's interesting that you should say that, Penny. Because I am prepared to give you something to think about in the days until I see you again. You should know that you have a choice between such a life and sharing my life which is relatively easy.

"Imagine for a moment, a house that is twice the size of your parents' farmhouse. It has gardens and lawns that are cared for by a gardener who has been with me since my grandfather owned the place. My housekeeper would be insulted if anyone else kept the house! She has been with me since Jeannine's death. She is that steadying influence everyone needs… a sort of guardian of one's feelings and a giver of unsolicited good advice that I needed when my own world fell apart around me! You would not have to do anything but enjoy the place!

"Whatever you need you have only to ask and it will be done for you. I think you will find that there are things I will provide for you that you did not even think you wanted!" And Kent laughed pleasantly.

Penny could only stare at Kent in disbelief. She had been promised things before. Sam had dreams. They had never been realized. They had been bubbles in the air that burst on the slightest pressure. This man spoke with confidence. These were no vain dreams. These were real luxuries she was being offered. They were hers for a simple assent. With a "yes" she could receive riches many women struggled vainly to achieve.

Kent interpreted her silence to mean that she needed more explanation of his wealth and the source of all these riches. He explained then about the world-wide company that he had established and which his inheritance from his grandfather had enhanced. He assured her that there would be time for them to travel together to any part of the world that was currently not at war. He assured her that his interest in the business would not consume him as it had done in the past because now he would have what he needed most... a wife for whom he had been searching for many years, seemingly in vain.

"Yesterday when we held our corporate meeting, I expressed my need to be relieved of some of my responsibilities. I will be semi-retired on September first. The full responsibility will be passed on eventually to whomever the board finds competent, on my recommendation, of course. But no matter whether I am in the business or out of it, my lifestyle is secure. My holdings and the investments have been wisely handled by my advisors, and these ensure us of security for our lifetimes and perhaps our children's lifetimes, as well!"

Penny spoke then in her soft voice, "Kent, I don't know what to say! You have offered me the world on a silver platter! I hope you won't be insulted by this question, but I must ask it for my own sake and my future happiness. Without this I would be miserable. My question is: Would I have you? Or, would you withhold your innermost being while giving me the outer shell? I cannot read minds; would you be willing to share with me your feelings, your wants, and your needs? I must know if I would have your most intimate self, Kent Hartman?"

Kent was thoughtful for a moment, not quite sure just why Penny had felt she must ask this. He thought that he had made it clear that everything he had would be hers! In his relationship with Jeannine, they had enjoyed intimacy. He wondered if Penny was saying that she had not!

Moving toward Penny then, Kent pulled his chair close to hers so that he faced her. Looking into her eyes he took both her hands in his, again aware of how small they were in his own. Without smiling, Kent concentrated on what he was about to say. He knew now that some of the pain Penny had experienced had probably come from someone, perhaps Sam, who had withheld himself from her. Could this lovely person have been subjected to the ultimate insult of a lack of intimacy between her husband and herself?

"Penny, I can assure you that I am offering you 'myself', whatever that may be! And, I expect you to give me 'yourself'. We shall be like that old fashioned rose we saw on our walk this evening. Remember how two roses were intertwined on one trellis? I will be the red one, bold and vigorous. I need your qualities to fulfill me, Penny, and I think you need mine to satisfy your needs. Am I right?"

Penny laughed at the analogy. She had loved the fragrance of the early roses that clambered over the trellis on the veranda. Their fragrance was rich because the white rose's perfume blended with that of the red rose in a special way.

"I'm not a clinging vine, Kent!" She laughed; so did he. "That's where the analogy ends! But, seriously, Kent, I believe you understand me. I can tell that you are very serious about this matter. I can tell you that I have wanted to be married to a Christian man with just your qualities. How could I find such a relationship? That was the problem. A woman cannot just go out and declare her needs. She must wait on the Lord because His timing is always perfect!"

"Even if there is a thirty-five year delay?"

"Even if!" Penny declared with her pleasant soft laughter.

Kent got up from his chair and went to the fireplace to stir the fire, placing the final log on the burning embers. Again, the sparks flew high before the dry log caught fire sending the odor of pine into the room. Kent watched the flames in silence. Penny sat quietly watching him. She got up from her chair and crossed the room to stand beside him. Together they watched the bright flames, dancing.

"Kent?"

"Yes, my beloved?"

"I have my answer for you."

"And what is your answer, my darling?" Kent turned to her, looking intently into her eyes.

"My answer is 'yes'! With all my heart, my answer is 'yes'!"

Kent moved a vase aside on the mantel of the fireplace and revealed a small jewelry box which he took and handed to Penny, now seated on her chair. Penny took the ivory case and when she lifted the lid, a gasp escaped her. "You remembered!" She breathed softly. There, on a velvet cushion was a beautiful platinum ring in the center of which was a magnificent amethyst surrounded by diamonds. Kent gently took the ring and placed it on her finger.

"Once when we were together (we were just children!), you told me that you loved amethysts and that your sister had lost your birthstone ring. With all my heart I wanted to replace it then and there. But, of course, I could not!"

"Oh, Kent, now is the best time to remember! Now is the happiest time of my life!"

Penny stood then and Kent moved toward her. Tenderly, he reached out to her and drew her toward him. Tenderly, he took her in his arms, enfolding her with his strength. He took his hand and reached out and swept the silver hair from her forehead. There was a damp curl on her right cheek, hiding the soft dimple there. With one long finger he swept it away, too, so that he could touch his lips to her cheek. A moan escaped him then; a deep sound from his throat that reached her ears and thrilled her.

Penny put her arms around his neck and answered his love sweetly. She first looked into his eyes, then, her gaze fell to his lips which she touched with her fingertips as softly as with a feather. When she lifted her eyes again she met his warm expression with her own. She closed her eyes as their lips met in their first kiss. So still, so precious was their time together that they both forgot everything but the sheer joy of their love for each other and the embrace that expressed it.

Presently, Kent walked with Penny to the door in the hallway that led to the stairway up which she would walk to her bedroom in the loft. Kent took her key and unlocked the door. Before he turned and left her to prepare for rest, he took her in his arms again. Murmuring against her soft hair those love words only lovers know, he kissed her gently.

"Good night, my darling!" He said. "Soon we will be together forever. Sleep well, my love!"

Penny closed the door and climbed the steps to her room. She leaned against the cool wood of the doorway. Her cheeks were very warm and she felt weak and very tired. As she hung the violet challis dress in the closet in preparation for bed, she hummed softly to herself the remembered melody of "Star Dust". She turned the amethyst ring toward the light and felt, within her breast, a satisfying warmth of feeling. She was faint with love.

Before she slept she turned to the Bible and read the words of the Song of Solomon. "My beloved is mine; and I am his!" She identified with the Shulamite maid. She felt within herself the desire to express to Kent her love for him in a physical way, but knew she could wait. By the grace of God; she could wait. Faint with her growing devotion to Kent, she tumbled into bed and spent a fitful night, tossing restlessly until morning when, exhausted, she slept; unmindful of Kent walking quietly past her door on his way back to the airport.

EPILOGUE

Kent and Penny were married on June 25, 1982.

News of their engagement only a month before had been greeted with surprise by Rob and Sue, as well as Aunt Mitzi. Rob needed some explanation which Penny gladly gave him and which he received with skepticism; that was his way. He made up for that by offering to help with the wedding plans. Sue offered her help, also, but Penny told them that the wedding would be a simple family affair held in Brighton Chapel with Pastor Dave officiating. Their attendants would be Jeff and Catherine Cranston. Afterward they would travel to Switzerland and Germany for their honeymoon.

Upon their return, Kent made arrangements to buy the farm for $150,000. He and Penny made plans to restore the farmhouse to its original 1880 charm. Penny and he hired a well-known landscape architect to transform Locust Hill into a green space with bike trails, new trees, a pond for fishing, and a pavilion for picnics by the stream. Tom and Ida became the farm's caretakers. The young people who were hired to care for the grounds called them "Gramma" and "Gramps". As Tom often said, he sure had a lot of grandchildren, considering he "never had no children of my own!"

With the purchase of the farm for more than its just price, Kent and Penny were satisfied that the family was taken care of. Sue was able to buy a small house for herself and her girls; Aunt Mitzi, although she received no inheritance from her brother's estate, could now enter a retirement home nearby and enjoy her latter years; Rob and Sara used their money to set Rob up in an advertising business that would ensure their future; Penny's sons, Bruce and Cliff and their wives used their inheritance to invest in the business Kent had begun and when Tom Drake retired a few years after Kent, they became the administrators of the company. They and their wives, Ann and Judy, enjoyed trips abroad and had children who came to fill the Pittsburgh mansion with their laughter and high spirits.

Kent, who had no children of his own, reveled in the pleasure of watching his step grandchildren grow and develop. He and Penny when they were not off to the farm or away on a cruise to St. Croix in the Caribbean or flying to Europe, found pleasure in each other and sometimes slipped away to the Cameron Estate Inn to occupy the lovely old-fashioned Dutch Country room with the fireplace where they had looked into each other's eyes and found there the love for which they had both longed.

For Kent the search had ended; for Penny the loneliness was over. As long as they lived they continued to renew their relationship through their intimacy and their mutual love for the Lord Jesus Christ.